Bow-on-Sea on the south coast was within comfortable distance of London. There the brisk trade of the seaside was conducted—ice-creams, lemonades, pleasure gardens. And there, also, existed the town's other life: the sharp-eyed inhabitants of the Market and Seaman's Rise, the gossips of Cato Gardens. No one could quite remember whether it had been Brendan Hamp who had first suggested moving to Bow-on-Sea. It might just as easily have been his wife, Ruth, or his younger sister, Polly. It might even have been one of his daughters, Hilary and Jean. Anyway, move to Bow-on-Sea they did, taking with them, unknowingly, the seeds of murder and violence.

Against the glitter—and squalor—of this bustling seaside town, Mrs. Butler has woven a highly original plot which has the reader guessing from page to page. What was the secret from the past that Brendan Hamp carried with him? Why was the cat, Hake, so savagely killed? Who had Miss Perlott, the old busybody next door, hoped to marry when death intervened? These are a few of the questions which only find answers when the final pages are reached.

Also by GWENDOLINE BUTLER

DEAD IN A ROW
RECEIPT FOR MURDER

THE
MURDERING KIND

by

GWENDOLINE BUTLER

GEOFFREY BLES
52 DOUGHTY STREET, LONDON

This book is fiction and all the characters in it are entirely imaginary

PRINTED IN GREAT BRITAIN BY
WYMAN AND SONS LTD., FAKENHAM

TO
DAVID AND LIN
BARLOW

PROLOGUE

"IT WOULD be a pity," said the policeman as he looked down upon the dead woman, "to take too poor a view of her murderer."

He paused and regarded the dead face on which lust, avarice and greed jostled with all other of the seven deadly sins for expression.

"It might have been his good deed for the day."

"I doubt if the Chief Scout would see it that way," said his subordinate, a young inspector of the Bow-on-Sea City Police.

"This is the end of a long trail for us, though. Do you remember the blue coat she is wearing? You ought to, you've seen it before, you know."

"I shall remember it now certainly." It was not a pretty sight although it had been, in its way, a pretty coat.

"Oh, you have seen it before. She bought it for the Big Day."

"Well, she's worn it for her big day all right."

The superintendent looked down at the dead face again and now it seemed to him that as well as all the vices all the virtues were marked there too, sympathy, affection, generosity, warmth—too much warmth.

"Poor thing," he said. "What a pity we didn't know her better. We ought to have done."

"Policemen don't get much chance."

7

"Three things ought to have told us about her. All the gossip, the singing on the sands and the bright, bright clothes."

"I don't know that they told me much. I never seem to see that sort of thing."

"She was a canary all right. I should have seen it earlier." He sighed. "And to think I once thought a canary was just a little yellow bird."

The house was very still about them. The neat clean curtains fluttered slightly in the hot breeze and the flowers in the garden outside sent a smell of sweetness through the open window. It was a pleasant place to live in though perhaps it had not been a pleasant place to die in, but no place could have been pleasant to die in the way this woman had done. She had died furiously, angrily, not able to believe that this could be happening to her.

"Bright little room really," said the younger policeman, looking round. "I like blue and yellow. Difficult to associate it with her."

"Well, she was gay enough." The superintendent's voice was grim.

"When I look at people like this I remember that I like to be alive." In spite of himself the younger man was sad. "Well, now I suppose we have to tell the next of kin."

"And you don't think the kin might walk right out and tell us? That lot weren't behind the door when knowing things were handed out."

"I suppose they could see how things were going. If we had our sins, then they must have had theirs—if they wanted to see them, but I can't help thinking that they wanted to be blind. Otherwise they would have noticed, well I suppose they would have noticed the preoccupations, the secrets, the absences, and the sense of energy diverted from its right channel, those were the things for them to see. But they didn't want to see them."

Outside the windows they could hear the sounds and smells of the beach. The holiday season was in full swing and the two detectives could watch girls in bright sun-dresses and light sandals, young men with dark sun-glasses and coloured shirts, children with buckets and spades—all the picture of a summer day. There was a sound of music and shouting from the pleasure ground close by.

"I suppose it's right she should die within sound of the beach," said the younger man.

"I've given up seeing justice in such events," said the other, "but I know what you mean. On the whole there have been three great milieus connected with all this . . . first the house, then the pleasure ground, and then the beach."

"Three places, and a woman associated with each of them, and all the time we knew that one of them was *the* woman, the woman behind the whole train of events."

"Well now we know which woman it was," said the superintendent from London. "And it was her. I should have seen it before." He looked down at her sadly. "Poor thing," he said sadly.

"And what about the other one?" said the local man. "Aren't you forgetting her?"

"Ah yes, the first one. Do you know I can hardly think back to the days when we didn't know the first one had been murdered, when we didn't know we had a case to answer."

And they were both silent. And as they stood silent

they could hear from outside the open window unmistakable noises of a crowd of people muttering in anger and alarm.

Although the case had played itself out in comparative obscurity now that there was hint of an arrest there had begun to be a feeling of anger and of a desire, somehow, for a revenge.

"They haven't heard about this new death," said Winter going to the window and looking out.

"Don't be too sure. You know how these things get about. Listen."

In the distance, above the cry of the ice-cream man and the music from the pleasure ground they could hear a newsboy shouting, "Murder, murder, new murder." The holiday-makers hurried to buy their papers, there was nothing like a good murder on a summer's holiday.

Anger, envy, malice and uncharitableness in holiday clothes were looking for a scapegoat.

CHAPTER ONE

A SMALL open yellow car followed a van round the corner of Seaman's Rise and stopped sharply. Too sharply. A bit black cat sitting in a cage was knocked from the back where it was angrily sharing a seat with a Boxer dog and a large, fair man, and hit the road. The cat swore nastily and so did the man.

"Damn you, Poll. I always said you were a bad driver."

The Hamp family were on the move. They were coming to live at Bow-on-Sea, the splendid resort on the south coast so very near to London. It was a family uprooting on a large scale. The pantechnicon parked outside their new house was packed with their furniture, and the little yellow car had Hake the black cat and Buster the dog and Brendan Hamp sitting in morose companionship, or had had until Hake fell out. Hake was in her cage, Buster was tethered and they had hated the journey, each other and Brendan. Did we have to move? said the expression on their faces, and this was a question which even the Hamps found it difficult to answer. They had left a perfectly reasonable house in Finchley, and they were now moving, perfectly unreasonably, to Bow-on-Sea. Whose idea had it been? When it came to the point neither Brendan Hamp nor Ruth his wife would admit to it. And it certainly hadn't started with the two Hamp girls, Jean and Hilary. So perhaps after all it had been due to pretty, witty Aunt Poll. Certainly the Hamp household had never moved before, remaining fixed even through the recent second marriage of Brendan, and the noisy growing-up of his two girls.

"Wouldn't be the first time Poll's had a bad idea," muttered Brendan Hamp as he crawled out of the seat he had so uneasily shared with the two animals. Buster at once moved over, but not particularly gratefully. "Look at that husband of hers. Not that I ever have. Poll, was it necessary for me to share a seat with those two beasts? They don't like me and I don't like them. They've been eating fish."

"That's the sea air," said Poll absently. She was Brendan's very much younger sister, although perhaps not so much younger as she appeared, and professionally she was known as Polly Parsons, a designer of women's underclothes, chiefly of those important garments known as foundations. They had certainly been the foundation of Poll who acted very prosperous and who, now that she had come to live with them, helped support the Hamps in the comforts they were used to but certainly couldn't afford. In private life she was Mrs. Tony Fisher but who Tony was and what and where he fished no one had ever discovered. But that he was one of the fish better left in the sea was Brendan Hamp's often stated opinion; he never had much opinion of his sister's judgment. Poll never gave any direct information but hinted at dark tragedy or broad comedy according to her mood. No one could give her the lie because she had lived since before the war in Canada and had only just come home. She had a fragile appearance but a tough nature. "You often think you smell fish round here but it's the sea really."

"That's going to add to the joys of life," grunted Brendan.

"Anyway it's not me that decided on the house," said Poll going back to an earlier point as she was apt to do. "Although, mind you, I think it's an excellent idea. I shall be able to go into sunsuits and swimming costumes as well as foundations, probably start a factory here. I'm bound to be a success. *You* saw the house and said it'd be a crime not to buy it. So you obeyed the dictates of law and order, as you usually do." She placed a slight emphasis on the last words and Brendan's lips tightened.

"You'll be dead duck one day, Poll, if you don't watch your tongue." He knew, or thought he knew, that she was thinking of the time during the war when the violence and antagonism to law had come to the surface in Brendan and he had almost killed a man; he had only escaped court martial because the other man had been willing to hush things up and because the battalion went overseas next day to Normandy. And there had been another occasion earlier, only perhaps Poll didn't know of this. It had been in 1940 just after Poll left the country. But there had been a domestic tragedy hanging over Brendan at that sharp time in history so perhaps he was to be excused.

"Better be a dead duck than a dodo," said Poll. "At least I've lived."

"So you keep hinting. I suppose your husband helped?"

"Whatever I may say about my husband, Brendan," said Poll sharply, "I can't see that there's any call for you to join in. I dare say he may have broken my heart but . . ."

"It wasn't your heart you complained of yesterday, Poll," Brendan reminded her, "but your furniture."

Poll looked at him then she burst into laughter; the pair eyed each other affectionately.

"Well maybe it was both."

"Did I hear the magic word furniture?" asked Ruth Hamp suddenly appearing in the road. She had come down earlier in order to receive the furniture and be, as she put it, ready for them. She now stood watching them, a tall, plump handsome girl. "You've got here at last. Almost given you up. How much have you broken and how many cars did you hit, Poll? My goodness, Brendan, what are those long red scratches on your face?" She looked at Poll in a questioning way as if after all perhaps Poll *had* hit one of those cars she usually so narrowly missed.

"That would be dear Hake's delicate claw," said Brendan thoughtfully, "she never did like me. Oh well, everyone has her taste, I suppose."

"Where is Hake?"

For answer Brendan went round the back of the car and picked Hake in the cage out of the road. He held up the cage. "She's a fierce customer, isn't she?" And indeed the large black cat glaring balefully between the bars of the parrot cage and angrily banging her head on the swinging perch was an intimidating spectacle. It did intimidate Buster who put down his head and howled. "Do you suppose I'm scarred for life?" went on Brendan. "Should I put on iodine?"

Brendan thought a good deal about medicine. He had to; he was the man behind the advertisements in the *Lancet*, the *British Medical Journal* and the *Doctor*; he wrote the magic words that sold the drugs to the trade, so he had a smattering of medical and scientific knowledge.

14

"Oh, you won't have a scar," said Poll, "or not much I dare say."

"You sounded just like one of my loving daughters. Where are Jean and Hilary by the way? Not helping with the move? How like them."

"Coming down later," said Ruth.

"Much later, I hope," said their devoted parent.

"As late as they can manage by train, I expect. Or in someone's car if Hilary can fix it."

"Yes, she's not one for spending her money. And they are coming together? I wonder which will be most ashamed of the other?"

"They get on better these days, and now that Hilary has stopped trying to look like the girl on the cover of *Vogue* and Jean given up looking like something on the cover of *St. Trinian's School Magazine* they both seem more normal." Ruth was laughing.

"There's room for improvement with Jean yet," said Poll critically.

"If," said their father, "you are hinting that Jean and Hilary are not exactly little joys about the house I can only say that I agree with you. Don't you think that from about fifteen to twenty-two are about the most tiresome years in a girl's life? For everyone, her parents and herself. But it comes and goes. Sometimes they are almost human beings, and act as though they thought I was one too—although that's rarer. However, Hilary, if she is to be believed, will shortly be leaving us to get married."

Poll looked thoughtful. "I have a definite feeling that you will not be losing a daughter but gaining a son."

"You mean they will *both* be coming to live with us?"

"I do."

"Well, it had occurred to me too, I must admit. Lucky we have a bigger house now. I wonder if I ought to have chosen a house large enough for Jean to use too?"

"Do you think she'll need it?"

"Well, she's just seventeen so I should think any minute now, wouldn't you? Of course, she is still at school, which usually has a retarding effect on people."

"The trouble with you two," said Ruth looking from one to the other, "is that I never know whether to believe you or not." Her big brown eyes had a puzzled look.

Her husband smiled at her. Whatever else he was worried about there was no doubt, in his mind at any rate, that his marriage was a great success. He thought back to the year he had got engaged and married to Ruth. They had met and married within a month after meeting at a very dull party given by the advertisers to the doctors. "Will you take on a soured old widower and two ghastly girls?" he had asked three years ago. "It's a risk. You'd always be wondering why the first marriage didn't take."

"Anyone's wife can die."

"She'd gone anyway. Dead to me, as they say in the books, long before. Rushed up to London to *him* and might have rushed back in the end I suppose considering what he was, but a bomb got her first. It was in *those* days you see."

"Don't be bitter."

"I'm not bitter. Just not very sweet in the mouth about it. But it's a common story."

"I believe that's what you don't like. You'd rather have an uncommon story."

"Yes, we do rather go in for the big tragedy in my family. Wait till you meet my sister Poll. She's had more tragic things *nearly* happen to her than all the heroines of Shakespeare—if you can believe her that is, which I never quite can. She's plausible though. So will you take on a family of lying egoists?"

And in spite of this Mr. Rochester and Jane Eyre wooing, perhaps because of it, because it was so unlike what she was used to in the bars of Chelsea and the King's Road, Ruth had taken them on. She had made a success of the marriage in a vigorous bouncing way. The girls began to love her and she made Brendan Hamp happy too. In her placid, determined way she was changing the Hamp family. She was a good cook and housekeeper and provided generously for everything. She was not a worrier, taking life as it came and making the best of it, but all the same lately she had been worried about Brendan; she knew that the ghost of his first marriage had not been exorcised. He was still punishing himself and her.

For a moment she and Brendan looked at each other, both of them sunk in the past. Then Ruth roused herself.

"Furniture," she said firmly, returning them to Scaman's Rise, Bow-on-Sea.

"The men have just started to carry the furniture in and you'd better keep an eye on them. I don't like the look of the one in the butcher's overall."

"Got his eye on the silver, eh?"

"More likely on Poll."

"What?" said Poll. "With you around?"

"Furniture," repeated Ruth.

"Right-ho," answered Brendan cheerfully, admiring her as she stood there. "Glad you've got that dress on, always brings us good luck, that dress. You were wearing it the time we came back from Paris stacked up

17

with scent and brandy and the customs looked like getting sticky and then they didn't."

"And I had it on the day the ceiling in the kitchen came down," said his wife with amusement. "But as you weren't there I suppose it doesn't count. Yes, it's a good dress but I think it must have shrunk."

Brendan smiled. There was no doubt that the dress *was* too tight, but then, damn it, the girl had the figure to wear tight dresses.

"Oh well, you can give it to Buster to sleep on—he'd love that." And he put an arm round her waist.

"Now come on, Brendan," said Poll. "Work, not play, you know. You two always like this?"

"No," said Ruth, sharply for her.

"What vulgar ways you've come back with," said Brendan.

"I went vulgar, dear," said Poll without animosity. She was fussing round the car like a pretty, sharp little animal. Her sister-in-law moved over slowly and gracefully to watch. "You didn't know me then, Ruthy. Luck for you."

"I wish I had known you all then. Seems to me I missed a lot not knowing all of you all these years."

"Perhaps, like measles, it's better to get us over young."

"You're so cynical, Poll, that's the only thing I've got against you Hamps, you're always so cynical. You're much better people than you give yourself credit for being."

"Credit, Ruth, my dear, is the one thing we always allow ourselves. I wonder you haven't noticed. By the way, did we pay all our bills before we left?"

"More or less, I should think," said Ruth with a

frown, but she was hardly listening. "Now we must unpack the car. I don't like the look on Buster's face. I think he might bite someone if we don't untether him fast."

"Well, do it yourself, dear," said Brendan nervously for he and Buster had no love for each other.

"Coward," said Ruth advancing. Buster leaned out and put out a long pink tongue and began to lick Brendan's hand. "That's right, dear, lick the master."

"Take him away, Ruth," said Brendan, backing nervously. "He'll get me yet."

Ruth and Poll seized Buster by the collar and dragged him into the house. He was quite willing to go and trotted along sheepishly.

"Do you do everything that man tells you?" asked Poll. She sniffed at the hand which had grasped Buster suspiciously. "Maybe they have been eating fish," she muttered.

Ruth's large oval face with its gentle ardent brown eyes looked puzzled. Poll sighed. She considered her sister-in-law a nice woman but slow, real slow.

"Oh well, yes I do, I suppose," Ruth answered. "Within reason." I doubt if you're strong on what's reason and what isn't, dear, thought Poll.

The two women were standing in the kitchen. It was quite empty except for the gas stove, a kettle and a teapot. Ruth had the kettle boiling as her sister-in-law gratefully observed. She lit a cigarette and leaned against the window.

"Shall we take Brendan out a cup and say he can come in now?" she suggested. Buster was sitting gloomily by the sink and clearly was in no mood to bite anyone, even his master. "I could do with one too. Don't you think that moving is soul destroying? I feel quite miserable, and heaven knows this isn't really my home. I used to feel quite terrible about it in Canada, and, my dear, we moved six times in one year. Still that had to be on account of . . ." And she fell silent. "Perhaps it's because one always seems to have dirty hands," she went on, looking down at her own.

"Oh well, a family removal like this is bound to be up-rooting."

"Come to think of it no Hamps ever lived by the sea before. We weren't all that struck on it—go and have a look at it now and then in a good summer, even a fort-night by it occasionally, but live by it, no."

"I really don't know why we did move," said Ruth.

"Oh, come off it, Ruth, you and Brendan are moving away from something more than just London." There was a moment's pause. "Aren't you?"

"Let's have a cup of tea, shall we?" And Ruth removed the kettle and warmed the pot. "I never met a girl like you for getting ideas."

"I haven't been a girl for years."

"It is true though that Brendan has got the most extraordinary notion. . . . No, I really can't tell you."

"You'd better. I'll strangle you if you don't after that beginning."

"Well, he's got the funny idea that someone didn't *like* us there."

"Really?" Was Poll being sarcastic?

Was Poll being sarcastic? Ruth couldn't be sure. "Now don't start that way of talking with me. I've got enough to cope with. Yes, he *did* think so, and in a big way I can tell you. Whatever he says now about not

20

knowing why he wanted to move he knew all right when he got on the train to Bow-on-Sea to look at the house here."

That's not quite what you said a minute ago, commented Poll to herself, but she let her sister-in-law go on talking without interrupting her.

"You know how it's been lately. . . . Brendan and I both felt the atmosphere, perhaps it wasn't any more than that. I don't know. So difficult to put your finger on. But you know there were tangible things. We simply couldn't keep the people who worked for us—the odd-job gardener, the man who helped with the car, even the window cleaner, they all upped and left." She looked puzzled. "I just can't make it out. Anyway, Brendan got it into his head that someone was starting talk about us, making us disliked."

She got out the cups and started to pour tea thoughtfully, then she shook her head, "No, I think he's made a mistake, it can't be that, but naturally he isn't very happy about it, so when he said let's move I encouraged it. And, of course, I like Bow-on-Sea and at the same time it's near to London. Healthy, too."

"Oh, I'm all for it," said Poll brightly but all the same she looked slightly taken aback. She was sufficient of a Hamp not to like anything that was bad for business and *talk* which, of course, meant unfavourable talk was certainly that, so perhaps this accounted for her look.

Brendan came into the kitchen carrying Hake who was poking at him with an angry paw.

"Why don't animals like me?" demanded Brendan. "I really think if Hake was my size he'd eat me."

"Oh, he's ever so gentle really," said Poll, patting

Hake's angry black head. "I don't say I'd keep him if he was mine because he's no beauty, is he, and all that fighting, but Jean loves him."

"Did the man I arranged to look at the garden turn up?" demanded Brendan, dropping Hake and the cage on the floor and seizing his cup of tea.

Ruth shook her head.

"Anyone else been around?" asked Poll. "Anyone for me?" She was very casual.

"Expecting anyone?" asked her brother, not in the least taken in by her manner. He knew his Poll.

"I thought Bert Gibbon might look in." If anything Poll was even more casual.

"That man." Bert and Brendan had had the bad luck to go to school with each other.

"Well, I thought he'd be a help. He could be a great help."

"Help? That man couldn't be a help if he'd got twenty hands and twenty eyes. He's a bore. What made you take up with a policeman I can't think."

"Oh, he isn't much of a policeman."

"He's as much of a policeman as I ever want near me." Brendan was not pleased. He and Bert had known each other since the age of five. Brendan had never liked Bert Gibbon and had made this clear. Bert perhaps felt the same but he was not so given to making his feelings apparent. On leaving school Brendan had gone to an art school thus starting in the first of the paths which were to make up his varied career, and Bert had gone into the police force where he had spent several years working with Inspector (now Superintendent) Winter as one of his team of assistants in criminal detection, but Bert had never quite pleased that ominous man—not nasty enough, his friends said—and he had in the end left the London police and retired to the force of Bow-on-Sea.

"There's no need to be nasty. And, anyway, I might be marrying him."

"And what about the husband you've already got?"

"Oh well, I could manage about that, dear, couldn't I? Be imaginative."

"That's a fine way for the future wife of a policeman to talk."

"He might be leaving the police force."

"What for? It's supported him for twenty years, hasn't it?"

"If you knew Bert better you'd be nicer about him."

"I was at school with him, wasn't I? And he was a boring little know-all then and he hasn't changed." Brendan produced his trump card, "And, what's more, Ruth doesn't like him, do you, duck?"

"I never said so."

"No, but I can tell."

"Furniture," said Ruth firmly, moving away. "We're moving, remember?"

The sound of a piece of their furniture crashing through the front door and the cheerful shout of "Easy there, mate," reminded them.

By the evening they were all exhausted, hot and tired. The day had turned unexpectedly warm and although this made them more tired it also cheered them up.

"Best house we've ever had," said Brendan at last, standing back and admiring his handiwork. He was proud of the house. "It's got character," he said.

It certainly had plenty of character, several characters in fact, not all getting on very well with each other, rather as if the builder had been a bit unsure of himself. The house was well built, there was no doubt about that, a great deal of concrete and solid stone had gone into its construction. From the front it was decidedly Georgian and it was this that had appealed to the Hamps who moved with the times and had given up admiring Jacobean half-timbering some time ago. At the back, where there was a glimpse of steel-grey sea, the house was Italian in feeling with a small loggia and a sterile-looking vine and even one mortified-looking statue of a boy with wings folded round him like rhubarb leaves.

"Do you suppose it's Peter Pan?" asked Brendan. But he was not really critical; it impressed him very much that he should have a statue in *his* garden.

"Pan, dear," said Poll. "Pipes of you know."

But the wings seemed to introduce an ecclesiastical not to say cimiterial note and it was difficult to identify the statue with Pan.

"Do you suppose the man who lived here was an artist?" asked Brendan.

"I know he wasn't," replied Ruth. "He was a master mason. Monumental, he said."

"Well, we've got a bit of his old stock," said Brendan. "All we want now is the rest of the tomb." He kicked at something heavy lying in the grass. "Maybe this is it."

"It's a head," said Poll, studying it. "Bronze, too, must be quite valuable." She wiped some of the dirt off with a handkerchief that she grabbed from Brendan's pocket.

The head when cleaned was clearly a portrait bust. As Poll worked away it could be seen to be a man.

"Must be old," said Poll, impressed. "Roman do you think? Couldn't be Greek, could it?"

"Shouldn't think so," said Brendan. "Still, you never know your luck."

He, too, began wiping away; even Ruth got quite excited.

"Oh, there's a beard," screamed Poll. "Supposing it's really valuable."

"Could be Renaissance," said Brendan, scrubbing away. He had a good look at what was emerging, then he threw his handkerchief down. "Damn it," he said. "Look at it, recognise the face? It's Edward the Seventh. Must have been made for his coronation, and it isn't even very like him." He turned it over. "Look, Birming-ham."

"You mean to say it isn't valuable?" said Poll, disappointed. "Well, what a shame. I like it though, I shall put it on that little shelf outside my room. I call it distinguished."

Brendan looked at the head, and even then felt, for a second, an irrational moment of foreboding. He didn't like the head. Then he looked round the garden. On one side he could see through a belt of trees the roof of a large, grey, stone house and on the other side a gay red roof of a little doll's-house chalet with green shutters and white walls.

"There's an awfully nice boy in the big house," said Ruth. "He helped me turn on the water here. Pity he got so wet."

"Don't see too much of him," suggested Brendan. "The thing I like about this place is that no one knows us here."

"Well, that won't last," said Poll. "You couldn't expect it to. And I never knew you be so keen on this incognito business before, rather the reverse in fact.

You in hiding or something?" She meant what she said. She had observed without pleasure her brother's behaviour lately, he was irritable, jumpy and alert, too alert. And now there was what Ruth had had to say. "Ruth's told me something," she said, glancing towards her sister-in-law who had wandered out of hearing and was cutting flowers for the house.

"I don't mind telling you if Ruth's started," said Brendan. "In fact I'd be glad to. But it's been much worse than I told Ruth. Not just a feeling. People were *making* talk about us. I'd hear snatches with my name in it, and then I was losing friends, neighbours seemed to avoid us. I may have exaggerated but something was there, I swear. There was bad talk going round about us."

"You ought to have gone to the police."

"Oh, yes, the police. Someone like old Bert I suppose," said Brendan sardonically. "They are such a help. They were before, weren't they?"

"I don't see that they did so badly with Moira. They found her, didn't they?"

"When she was dead."

"It wasn't their fault. And she had left you anyway."

"That's right, she had, you know all about it, don't you? But not quite all. You weren't in England, you'd just left for Canada. There were one or two little things I didn't tell you about at the time. If you want to know I think the old business with Moira and *all* that went with it, is what the talk was about. That's why I had to get Ruth out. The police always had it in for me over that business, they used the words fraud and embezzlement, well maybe they were right, but I didn't know at the time, did I? Not at the beginning, anyway. And

God knows I've kept my feet straight and out of trouble since then, but the police haven't forgotten. You ask Bert, he knows all about it you can bet, he was a London copper in those days. And I wasn't going to the police— I'm not sticking my neck out for them to shoot at."

"You're mad," said Poll.

"I can tell that you two feel at home," said Ruth, walking towards them, "because you are quarrelling."

From the little chalet came the sound of a strong, powerful voice singing, it was a deep voice, yet with lighter tones in it, which made it difficult to tell whether it was the voice of a man or a woman.

An upper window in the house was opened and a large fair head popped out. The first voice had stopped and another one had taken up a song. This voice seemed familiar in a puzzling way to the Hamps.

The unnaturally fair head, bushy with curls and a little fringe, was poked farther out of the window.

"Didn't disturb you I hope? I've got to do my practising."

"Oh no," said Brendan, "we enjoyed it." He listened to the singing and the sound of a band. "You having a party in there?"

"Oh no, that's my sister."

"You're a talented family."

"Oh, we're not a family, we're a clan. I'm a Cresset. You've heard that name I don't doubt. If not I'll have to have a word with our agent."

In spite of themselves the Hamps were impressed. The Cresset family had been one of the great names in Music Hall and the theatre for generations.

"Used to be conjurors and jugglers, then dancers, we run to voices now," said Gypsy, filling in detail for them.

27

"We haven't had a real straight dramatic talent yet though," she added wistfully. "I'd have loved it myself but I haven't got the looks and then there's not room for a voice like mine, gets a laugh you see when I'm trying for the big scene." She sighed. "Now the girl who could have done it is my sister. I'm Gypsy, you won't have heard of me, I sing in the chorus and pretty far back, but I expect you've heard of my sister Cresta?"

"Oh, yes," said Ruth.

"Good lord, is she still singing?" asked Poll.

"Now there's a voice," said Gypsy, glaring at Poll. "Real class to it. And she could have gone on the legit. stage you know, but she chose not to. 'Gypsy,' she said, 'it's my duty to the family to go where the big money is,' and she did. She's been on a wonderful tour —Australia, South Africa, everywhere. She's flying home from the Cape, coming through Brussels. She's a lucky girl. All I ever do is to catch the fast train up to Victoria and I'm always train sick. But, of course, I haven't got Cresta's looks." She sighed again. This seemed to weigh on her mind. "What did you say your name was?" She was looking at them with interest.

"We're called Hamp," volunteered Brendan.

"Hamp," said Gypsy consideringly and with emphasis as if she had heard *that* name somewhere before. "Oh, are you?"

"What of it?"

"Oh well, nothing, it's just that I'd heard . . . You don't look like I expected."

"We don't?"

"Oh, of course, it's only talk I've heard. You can't take any notice of gossip, can you? And some people will say anything." She ran a hand through her hair. "Remember what they say about sticks and stones will break your bones but *names* will never hurt you."

She waved at them and drew back into the house.

Brendan was very white. "I'm not so sure," he said in a slow voice. "I think words and names *can* hurt you. The wound can go very deep."

He looked despairingly at his wife and sister. "But, God, what is it they say of us?"

Ruth took his hand. She, too, was not herself. Poll drew slightly away from them and looked dispassionately at Brendan. She had heard a strange note in his voice. Was her brother, she asked herself, really a sick man?

CHAPTER TWO

THERE WAS the sound of a taxi drawing up and then the shriller sound of voices arguing about the fare.

"The girls," said Brendan. He sat down on the grass and took out a cigarette. Perhaps his hand shook a little. "Come home, as always, dear things, just at the wrong moment." He took a long time lighting the cigarette. "And in a taxi, too. Why? I can't afford taxis, why should they?"

"I expect Hilary paid," said Ruth soothingly.

"That's just what they seem to be arguing about. Got a good deal of luggage, haven't they?"

The two sisters came up the garden path towards them. Hilary, a tall fair girl with a tawny skin and deep blue eyes, hidden now behind dark glasses, was first; she was carrying a pile of hat-boxes and a very small suit case. Behind her, bearing what she could carry of the luggage, walked her young sister Jean. She was as tall as her sister but a good deal plumper and not so pretty, there was less humour in her face and more anger—she was very much her father's daughter.

"You incognito, Hilary?" asked Brendan, looking at her dark glasses.

"Thought we all were," said Hilary and took off the glasses. "Shut the gate, Jean."

The gate banged hard and a good deal of blossom fell off the spring flowers.

"In some books," said Brendan, "you would be said to have burst in."

"Damn books, Dad," said Hilary.

"I'm glad I didn't give you an expensive education," answered her father. "Or now I should have to say what a lot of money I'd wasted."

"I never see what education does for a girl," observed Ruth.

"No, dear, but then you are a natural primitive."

"I don't know what you are talking about."

"Exactly what I mean. Well, girls, had a good day?"

"Oh, so so," said Hilary, kissing her father and counting her hat-boxes.

"She means that she bought a new hat and it cost more than she could afford, more than she had, in fact, and now she's not sure if it suits her," said Jean speaking for the first time and with asperity.

"You know, dear, you're in danger of developing into a character, and you know what *that* means. Something very nasty. No one in England is ever called a character unless they are downright unpleasant and quite often not very clean either. In fact, now I come to think of it, smell and a bit of dirt are essential to a character so perhaps you don't qualify as you seem quite clean." He turned to Poll. "Tell me, what do they call a character in Canada?"

"Oh, I don't think they have them," answered Poll absently.

"They're bound to have, but I suppose, very naturally, they didn't come your way."

"Well, if they smelt I'm glad they didn't. You trying to be rude to me?"

"I don't know why it is, Dad," said Jean thoughtfully, "but when you haven't been working you seem to suffer from a rush of words to the mouth. I reckon you need to work at advertising, it acts like the letting of blood. For spleen. See Robert Burton." Then she added, "If you've ever heard of him."

"He's an actor, dear, isn't he?" asked Ruth. "I didn't know he'd been ill."

Brendan eyed Jean. "I'm sorry to think that I'm still paying for *your* education—it isn't doing you any good."

"Well, you won't be paying so much at the new school, will you? So cheer up. As a matter of fact it's a nuisance to me to have to move school just now but you wouldn't think of that."

"There's a very nice boy next door," said Ruth, as if she hoped this would please Jean.

"That doesn't interest me."

"What about you, Hilary," said Brendan. "Any interest to you?"

"I'm engaged, father," said Hilary patiently. "I keep telling you."

"So you do. Anyway, you'd probably be too old for him."

"Oh, no," protested Ruth, "as if that mattered."

Hilary gave a scream and leapt forward. "That blasted cat's been sick on my hat. She ought to be put down."

"I don't think she's healthy," said Poll, "I'm always saying so."

"Oh, it was probably the car," said Ruth.

"Poor old Hake," said Jean tenderly picking up the cat and nursing it, "do they feel car sick? You are mean, Hilary."

"Jean's coming on," observed Hilary, "a tender and

womanly heart beats beneath that bleak dress—which is a spiritual gym tunic. Can't you do something about her clothes, Ruth?"

"Something to have a heart," said Jean. "More than you have, hard as nails."

Hilary smiled with the complacent air of one who has often been assured otherwise. Ben, her fiancé, she felt, knew better than Jean about her heart.

"And if Ben's said otherwise," said her sharp-witted sister, "you can take it from me he's biased. He's a fool, anyway."

"Just because he doesn't read Kafka . . ."

"Kafka," said Jean with scorn. "How like you to think that *Kafka*'s important—I finished with him months ago."

"You talked about him enough."

"The only way you'd ever heard of him, I suppose."

"You know it *is* her gym tunic," observed Poll who had been studying her niece closely. "What do you do with your dress money?"

"Yes, what do you do?" asked Brendan. Money and its disposal always interested a Hamp.

Jean flushed. "I've spent it," she said.

"Can't see any sign of it."

"Undies and things."

"In the circumstances I shall have to take your word for it."

"I haven't seen any undies," said Hilary, "and she borrowed my nylons—not that I could wear them afterwards. Probably spent the money on a set of Dostoevsky. Might teach her to cut her toe-nails. Oh," she broke off and added with an outraged air, "you've kicked me. I always said she was violent, Dad."

Ruth led her warring family into the house where already an air of comfort had taken the place of the mess of removal. The sitting-room was the most prepared room in the house and here someone, Poll perhaps, had placed great bowls of jonquils and freesias so that the whole room was scented.

Brendan looked round thirstily. "A drink would be nice."

"Get the drinks, Hilly," said Ruth.

"Why is it always me that gets the drinks? Why always me? Am I supposed to be specially skilled or something?"

"Your job, love," said Ruth with an air of wonder.

"Look, it isn't that sort of bar. He's a barrister, not a barman." Hilary, although of a frivolous appearance, was a frighteningly competent secretary and worked in a nest of lawyers in Gray's Inn. "I wish you'd get that straight." Did Ruth really get muddled? Hilary was far from sure. "It's really luck for me to have such a good job—they hate women working in chambers really —that's what they call the place they work."

"Funny name," said Ruth idly. "Nasty really."

"Ruth, really. Anyway, my man likes to have me because I'm a really good typist. But his bar has *nothing* to do with drink."

"Got everything to do with it, I should think," said Brendan, "judging by what I saw of him."

"Daddy, you've never seen him. That was his junior."

"Well, your man must be Methuselah."

"They're the same age." Hilary was getting sulky.

"Can't be junior then, can he? You want to learn the English language."

"Oh, you lot will never know anything. Junior means he's not a Q.C., and that means . . ."

"Oh, spare us what it means," said Jean.

The front door bell rang loudly, and then, as no one answered it, rang again.

"We aren't in," said Brendan.

Poll and Ruth looked at each other. "I bet I know who that is," said Poll.

"Betty Perlott," said Ruth, and she giggled.

"And who's the amusing Miss Perlott?" demanded Brendan.

"She's the Bents' housekeeper; they live in the big house the other side of us. Mr. Bent's an engineer, always away, and he has this housekeeper to look after the house and his boy. I told you about *him*, such a nice boy. But the housekeeper is the biggest old Nosy Parker you ever saw. I knew she'd be round to have a look."

"She's had about twenty looks already," said Poll.

"We've got lovely neighbours," said Brendan. "A mad woman on one side and an inquisitive old hen on the other."

"Oh, I don't think that old Gypsy's mad, just . . ."

"She's theatrical. I know."

The door opened and a little woman stood on the threshold.

"Oh, I knew you'd be too busy to open the door, so I said, just pop in, Betty, and see if help's needed."

Her eyes were moving alertly round the room while she spoke; if she missed any vital information it wouldn't be her own fault. "You have got everything nice. There's a bit of dust on that walnut table though." And she whipped a little yellow duster out of her pocket and gave the table a shine. "I can't help being house proud," she said gaily.

"Even in someone else's house," muttered Brendan, half but only half, under his breath.

Miss Perlott ignored this however.

"Let me know if there's anything I can do for you, won't you? I like to be neighbourly. Of course, I'm pretty busy. I have a young lad to look after; well, you know him, don't you, fancy me forgetting; made quite an impression on him, you have. Of course, I practically brought him up. Been quite a mother to him. Used to be such a nice, neat, tidy little boy, but *now*—still, army life changes a boy, doesn't it, and he's just finished his army training. Of course, we all read psychology these days and so we are all broadminded but I wonder sometimes . . ."

"What's Gypsy Cresset doing running round her garden at this hour?" wondered Ruth who was looking out of the window.

A look of anxiety crossed Miss Perlott's face. Where was it best to be? she was asking herself. Was she missing something?

"I think it *is* her own hair," said Hilary walking over and joining in. "But it might be a wig. . . ."

With a muttered apology Miss Perlott was gone.

"Is Gypsy really in the garden?" said Ruth. "There's always a chance, isn't there?"

"And her hair usually does look like a wig," said Poll.

Hilary sank down on a chair and kicked off her high-heeled shoes.

"Don't relax too soon, girls," said Brendan who had gone to the window. "There's a nice chubby, handsome young man in an open-neck shirt and looking, Jean, like the young Shelley."

"'That's no draw to me," snarled Jean.

"The young Dylan Thomas then."

"It's Stephen, I suppose," said Poll getting up quickly and patting her hair.

But when he came into the room Stephen seemed a nice, plump, dreamy young man, not perhaps much like a poet either.

"I hope you don't mind me calling so soon. I saw Miss Perlott coming in, and I thought she might have been worrying you."

"She didn't worry us much, she didn't stay long," said Brendan. "She found she had to hurry off."

"She's pathological I'm afraid. I'm fond of her in a way, I've known her so long, but she's getting worse, she can't stop prying into everything."

"Yes, she had a little pry here," said Brendan, "but don't worry." He was angry though.

The room they were sitting in had been decorated blue by the last owner, the monumental mason.

"This colour makes me feel like the eyes behind a blind man's spectacles," said Brendan irritably.

"It's Madonna blue," said Ruth with an air of knowledge.

"Oh, not quite, do you think?" asked Stephen seriously. "Not in the best Florentine pictures. Something a little deeper?"

"Let's just call it blue, shall we?" said Jean.

"Well, I would myself," agreed Stephen.

"Have you ever seen a Florentine picture?" asked Jean suspiciously.

"I have, as a matter of fact," said Stephen. "There's some in the gallery here."

"I believe there's plenty in the National Gallery," said Jean. "I expect you can afford the fare."

"I have seen them, as a matter of fact, but I wonder if you have?"

"She hasn't," said Hilary. "I can tell you that. She's been going around saying that nothing before Cézanne is worth looking at."

"There's a lot in these early fellows," said Stephen. "You ought to go and look at them. I'll take you tomorrow."

"Oh, she'll be at school tomorrow," said Ruth.

"No, I won't be, I start on Monday. I think I'd like to come. Thank you for asking me," she added primly.

"Well, I hope everyone will forgive me," said Brendan, "if I go to bed. I'm tired."

"Yes, I must go too," said Stephen hastily.

Slowly the Hamp family made its way to bed. Ruth sighed as she went up behind Brendan. "Sometimes I think Brendan's getting old," she said miserably.

"Oh well," said Poll, unwilling to pursue the subject. She had never known how much her sister-in-law knew of Brendan's earlier troubles.

"He's acting odd," said Ruth. "It isn't very nice for me." Then she noticed that Jean and Hilary were close behind. "Oh, Jean, you can borrow that white hat of mine for the trip to the Picture Gallery, if you like."

"Oh thanks," said Jean looking pleased. She followed Hilary into the bedroom they were going to share. It was a pretty little room decorated in pink and white with curtains of clear blue silk. Hilary had chosen everything. There was only one dressing-table and Hilary made for this at once. She sat in front of the mirror and anxiously examined her new hat. It was rather like a flower-pot with a big striped bow in the front and Hilary looked enchanting in it. Evidently she thought so herself because after a minute she put it down and sighed with pleasure. "Suits me, you know," she said. Then she frowned. "Which is more than that white hat of Ruth's does *you*. I don't know why she's lending it to you. Oh my, what a mad house we are. Madder than ever."

"I didn't notice." Jean was arranging her books in the window-seat.

"No, you wouldn't, but we are. And there's been something funny lately, hints, undercurrents. Wonder if it's due to Poll? Were we like it before Poll came? I can't remember."

"Oh, you're imagining things."

"Not me. I never do," said Hilary with conviction. "I can't. All the imagination in this family goes to you and Dad."

"I don't think Dad liked Stephen," said Jean in an abstracted way.

"Oh, Dad's always been a bit of a cave man," said Hilary easily. She had observed this early in her life and it did not worry her. "Bound to be with his history."

"I don't know what you mean."

"Oh well," and Hilary laughed, "and you're the one who reads books. Think of Freud. The patriarch stuff, resenting the young men, any men really. *You* know."

"I see." Jean looked thoughtful.

"Oh, you mustn't take it too seriously," said Hilary, the hard and worldly-wise. She didn't like the look on her young sister's face. "It's nothing big really. Anyway I *hope* not. I dare say he'll shake it off quite normally when I marry Ben, if I *do* marry Ben. It's just that you're so used to seeing everything in books and not in real life that it's shaken you."

"Just life will do," said Jean mechanically. "Your style's awful, Hilary."

"Life then. . . ."

Hilary tucked herself comfortably into her bed and thought about Ben whom, after all, she probably wouldn't marry, and also about the new young man she had in mind whom she would marry if she could, and then she slept happily. Hilary never worried.

But Jean lay in bed without sleeping, she lay looking into the dark and wondering. Something was going to happen to the Hamps.

"We're just an ordinary family," she told herself desperately. Hake crawled up on to her bed. She put out her hand to stroke the dark fur and as she did so she knew they were both afraid.

CHAPTER THREE

JEAN DID not go to the Picture Gallery with Stephen the next day, nor for many days afterwards. Something always seemed to go wrong, something always went wrong with Stephen's plans; he was that sort of person as they were beginning to learn. Events always seemed too much for him and he was perpetually at the mercy of mechanical objects which fascinated and defeated him. But he always rose to the surface and took up again almost where he had left off.

In the weeks since their arrival the Hamps had settled down into a routine. Hilary and her father got into the little yellow car and drove rapidly to London each day, Jean went to the local big girls' school (which rather to her surprise she liked) and Ruth and Poll managed the house and gossiped with each other. Poll was off and out most of the day—she had discovered a small and almost derelict clothing factory near the sea front and she was playing with a plan for reopening it and making swim suits and beach clothes in it. There was also a tiny flat attached where the caretaker had once lived and where, if all went well, Poll thought *she* might live. All this seemed to mean Poll travelling around a great deal and being very gay. Not much progress was made towards actually starting up work, but as Poll said the factory couldn't run away. Meanwhile she talked gravely about acetates, the new synthetics and experiments.

While all this went on Ruth was left to herself a good deal, but she never seemed to mind nor be lonely and they always found her cheerful.

Eventually Jean made sure of her expedition by arranging all the details herself and giving Stephen careful instructions, so that she didn't think even he could mistake the day, muddle the time or find he had urgent things to do elsewhere. She had read a number of books on early Italian paintings and thought that she might now show to advantage. At any rate she could use the name Berenson with advantage and she had already observed that this went a long way. Stephen was the first young man she had ever wished to impress but she knew she wanted to hold her own with him.

She crammed the borrowed white hat on her head, took out Hilary's best white handbag and set off down the road in the sun of a Friday (half-day from school) afternoon.

Gypsy was sunbathing in her garden enjoying the heat of early summer. She waved brightly. In spite of her inauspicious beginning Gypsy had managed to wriggle her way into a sort of friendship with all the family except Hake and Hilary. She had a way with her all right when she chose. Even Brendan pretended to forget what she had said to him the day they first met, and bore her with a long-suffering air. He saw a lot of her because she was constantly begging lifts to London in the car, where she established herself in the back seat with considerable satisfaction and either did singing exercises or went to sleep. Whichever she did she angered Hilary. When she was awake she talked constantly of her great problem, which was that her voice, always a deep one, was each month, each year, getting deeper. As she regarded Brendan, on account of his job, as a sort of doctor, she peppered him with questions. "What's the latest in the *Lancet*?" she would ask. "Anything that could help me? It's a tragedy really, here I am with the temperament and poise to sing *Tosca* or *Carmen* and me voice getting ready to sing *Ivan the Terrible*. You don't think I'm changing my sex, do you?" she would add, dropping her voice nervously. "Haven't had any other symptoms." Brendan very rarely answered her questions except once to recommend arsenic. "But that's a poison," shrilled Gypsy. Brendan reminded her that it whitened the skin and cleared the voice. "I don't want to be singing with the angels," muttered Gypsy and for some time after that she kept her worries about her voice to herself.

Today she was at home resting—rests alas were getting more common in Gypsy's theatrical life—and was ready for a gossip.

"Hallo, Jean," she said. "Out for a walk, eh? Cresta's coming home tomorrow." Another curious thing about Gypsy was her relationship with the mysterious sister—Cresta was always said to be coming home but so far she had never appeared. Couldn't face life with Gypsy was the Hamp opinion. "I've had that nasty Perlott woman hanging round me. Trying to find out about Cresta. Think she'd got something better to do," said Gypsy, "than making bad blood between sisters. Still I settled her," she said, putting her feet up comfortably, "she won't come near me again. Or not for a bit. Someone ought to shoot her. Dare say they will some day. You going through Mariners' Market? Hold on to your bag then. They'd take your back teeth from you there if they thought there was a sale on, *and* you wouldn't notice until you came to have a chew. Watch out for the Irishman, he's the worst." And she settled back with closed eyes to dream of Cresta.

Jean hurried down Seaman's Rise and turned into the market. It was a broad short street of shops and stalls and barrows leading to the sea. It was always crowded and always noisy. The Post Office was on one side, a large café on the other and the Picture Gallery, the pride if not exactly the joy of Bow-on-Sea, was round the corner.

There was no sign of Stephen, which did not surprise Jean. She mounted the short flight of marble steps and stood looking at the sea until Stephen came hurrying down the hill. He ran up the broad steps towards her, then stopped short.

"Didn't recognise you in that hat," he said, "thought you were Ruth for the moment."

The entrance hall was dim and quiet and smelt strongly of the black and green rubber which covered the floor. The first room was large and almost empty: a group of schoolgirls, from her own school, Jean noticed, were glumly listening to a lecture from a young woman on the 'school of Cimabue', which, judging from the comments passed among them, they seemed to consider a kind of reform school; a large black man was studying the catalogue and eating milk chocolate, and two elderly women were having a quiet sit-down and talking about operations.

"We'll go into the Italian room first," said Stephen, leading the way forward and tripping over one of the women's feet. She quietly removed them and went on talking about gall-stones.

The Italian room was of elegant proportions and the pictures in their gilt frames rested upon a pale green damask paper. It was empty except for an attendant reading a daily paper.

"Come and see one of my favourite pictures," said Stephen and he pointed out to her a large painting of a square-faced Madonna sitting by an open window nursing a placid but plain baby. "See the characteristic pose? And the way the baby is not *quite* cross-eyed? Typical of that school. It's by Titian."

"It says Tintoretto underneath," said Jean doubtfully, "but perhaps the picture has been moved," she added quickly.

The attendant, who had of course been listening to everything while doing his football pools, moved up to them. "That picture hasn't been moved for years. I doubt if we could move it now, sir, without it collapsing. Rotten bad canvas. And it's always said Tintoretto." He paused to make his effect. "And I'll tell you what, it ain't by Tintoretto. Never has been. *Would* we have a Tintoretto in a place like this? No. And it's not. Painted in Paris in 1900, I should think." He paused again. "And I shouldn't trust the little Fra Angelico nor the Bassano."

"Isn't anything genuine?" asked Stephen.

The attendant was thoughtful. "I don't *believe* the little Bellini is genuine, but it always might be. He painted a lot, stands to reason he must have had his off days. But I doubt it. Now I tell you what is genuine, that's the little Landseer in the end room. No doubt about it. You have a look. Nasty, mind you. Still, it's genuine."

"But it says in the catalogue that this picture is by Tintoretto," said Jean, who had been studying that production. "It's not honest,"

"Ah now, you read it again. See? It says *attributed* to Tintoretto. That's a snarky way of saying that as far as they know Tintoretto never set eyes on it."

"You seem to know it all," said Stephen.

"I've been here ever since it opened. I've picked things up. Bound to. No money in it though. I'm the poor relation, I am. Not like my brother down at the fun-fair."

Stephen laughed, he could see the joke against himself. "Lesson's over for today, Jean, we might as well go home."

On the way out they passed a picture which they had not noticed before. It was hanging in a little corridor leading to the Modern French room.

"Now even I know that's not genuine," said Stephen.

"A copy of a copy," said the attendant appraisingly, "that's what you might call that."

"Unfairly perhaps," said Stephen.

Jean looked puzzled. "What is it?"

"Well, what is it? Look at the picture."

"They're bathing, it's a sort of picnic."

Inside its thin black frame the picture, even though it was a reproduction, was vivid and spirited.

"It's a copy of Manet's 'Picnic', which in itself is set out to follow the design of Gorgione's 'Concert Champêtre'. Lovely, isn't it? Caused a sensational scandal in its day."

"Did it?" said Jean, untouched by any precognition of the future.

"Lovely though. Wish I could paint like that. I tried to teach myself before I went in the army. But I'm no good."

"It must have been terrible for you in the army."

46

"Oh no, it wasn't. I didn't think I'd enjoy it but I did. A man's glad to do something like it. And it was in the Engineers. Very interesting. Of course I wasn't very good at that either. I'm glad I went in before going to the University—if I do go, that is."

"Oh, you will."

"I don't know. Lately I've been thinking I'd rather go straight out into the world."

"Like your father, I suppose?" asked Jean doubtfully.

"Well, not so far into it as father. Let's forget it. Let's talk about pictures. I like Renoir, don't you?"

"Yes." But Jean was doubtful. "No."

"Oh, little girl's taste. He's wonderful. The only person who could do that sort of pearly fleshy gleam like him is Ingres."

But Jean had never even heard of Ingres.

"It's amazing how one's tastes change, isn't it? Now a few months ago all I really enjoyed were landscapes—Cézanne and so on. Now I can see how lovely the human body is. So I enjoy all the other paintings I didn't enjoy before. It's the same in music, I used to find opera dull—now I could listen to the human voice singing all the time."

"You would do if you lived next door to Gypsy like we do," said Jean drily.

"Did looking at pictures do that for me?" said Stephen half to himself, not listening to her. "Or what was it?"

"There's someone waving to you from the other side of the street," said Jean, not reluctant to drag him back to her presence again. She pulled irritably at the white hat.

"Oh, that's my friend Ish Murphy," said Stephen.

"Oh, an Irishman. I can't do with all these brooding

47

Celtic fires—all so gay and manly on top and all so sensitive and deep underneath."

"Well, I wouldn't call Ish a brooding Celt exactly but there's plenty of fire in him all right."

"What is he?"

"He's what's called a building contractor," said Stephen with a faint giggle; "that means he does what he can where he can for as much money as he can. Don't despise money, Ish doesn't. But he's got other interests. He's an existentialist, the only one in Bow-on-Sea."

"He must find it lonely."

"Oh, Ish is never lonely."

"Too many other interests, I suppose."

They passed on the other side, with Ish still waving at them.

When they were nearly home Jean saw her father walking towards them, and she knew that her lovely gay afternoon was over. He came up to them with a nod.

"Wondered where you were. Hello, Stephen. Your housekeeper is looking for you. I've just met her. She seems angry. You went out without telling her something about the laundry."

With a muttered good-bye Stephen hurried forward to where Miss Perlott could be seen at the gate.

"You don't like him, do you, Father," said Jean; "Stephen, I mean."

"Let's not put it like that," said Brendan with controlled irritation. "Let's just say he's too perfect for me. There he goes, young, handsome (I suppose you would call him handsome?), clever, faultless. That's it, you know. I'd like him better if he had a fault."

"Something's happened, hasn't it, Dad?" asked Jean. Her face was white.

Brendan nodded. "Yes, I was coming to look for you; your mother thought . . ."

"My *mother*!"

"Ruth I mean." Brendan was flustered. It occurred to Jean that in moments of crisis he genuinely confused his two wives.

"Tell me what's happened?"

"It's the cat. She's had an accident. Someone's killed Hake."

In the distance, by the gate to the Bents' house they could hear Stephen's voice raised angrily.

Brendan listened, then laughed bitterly. "I take it all back. I *do* like him. He *has* got a fault. He's got a temper."

Jean burst into tears.

CHAPTER FOUR

"NOT A bad old cat," was Hake's epitaph. Brendan buried him and Jean wept bitter tears. The cat had come to them as a broken-down old stray and Jean had nursed him and loved him; he had not returned the affection because he was not that sort but if he had trusted anyone he had trusted Jean.

"The cat wasn't killed accidentally," said Brendan sombrely next morning. "He was hit on the head deliberately. I'm sure of that. I had a look."

"Why would anyone do that?" said Poll. "Just a little old cat." She drank some coffee.

"Someone who doesn't like us. Just malice."

"Seems awfully methodical for malice," said Poll putting her finger on an important fact unwittingly. "Banging the cat on the head and then putting it away tidily in the dustbin like that. Funny."

Each of the family sitting round the breakfast table was summing up the situation and each thought that they could put a name to the killer of Hake. But only Jean put it into words. "That old beast Perlott," was all she said.

"We don't know it was her," pointed out Brendan. "Mrs. Buckett found the cat in the dustbin, that's all we do know really, and if she hadn't we might not know the cat was even dead yet. After all it's often gone off for days."

"And the bins get emptied today," said Hilary, "so it might have been some time before we wondered about

Hake if Buckett hadn't found the body. Good old Buckett."

"I'm sure it was old Perlott," said Jean; "she told me she hated cats, and she's a nasty person, the only person round here who would kill a cat just like that and then put it away in a bin. She's mad about hygiene, you know she is."

"There's a flaw in that argument somewhere," said Brendan in a worried way, "if I could put my finger on it. I think I'd better talk to Mrs. Buckett."

"It's Beckett really," said Ruth.

"Well Beckett or Buckett it's all one to me. Is she here now?"

Ruth nodded. Mrs. Beckett was in the kitchen. She was a cheerful and energetic worker much sought after and as she passed through most of the houses in Seaman's Rise in the course of the week she knew a good deal about everyone and everything. She refused however to offer an opinion on the death of Hake and merely muttered darkly and said cats would be cats.

But if indifferent to the fate of Hake and her own name she had demands of her own to make.

"Can I have another bottle of Sharpazone?" she said firmly. "You're out of it again. I always like my ladies to keep Sharpazone, and that bottle that we had yesterday has all gone. It bleaches everything and kills all the bacteria. Says so on the label."

"So it should," said Brendan, "neat bleach will kill anything, I should think." He got to his feet. "Come on, Hilary, we must go."

"Well, put the top up, will you? How can I be expected to look decent at work when I travel in that windblown monster."

"You could go up by train."

Hilary did not answer.   She had no intention of paying out good money on the train fare.   But Brendan knew.

"Mean, my girl, that's your trouble."

"I'm saving up. . . ."

"Don't tell me, so that you can get married.   Is Ben saving too?"

Hilary was silent.

"Anyway, you haven't been seeing so much of him lately, have you?"

Hilary grunted.   She was putting on her lipstick. "Can we have the top up?" was all she said.

"If we have the top up it stifles our passenger at the back," said Brendan mildly.

"That'd be a pleasure," said Hilary.   For of course the passenger was Gypsy.   Hilary said that Gypsy must have been the passenger the insurance companies had in mind when they thought of the original third-party risk.   "She makes us so conspicuous.   It isn't so much the way she looks.   I could forget about that when I'm not actually looking at her, but it's her singing.   She's getting odder and odder.   Why must she sing in the back of our car? And what's more, she don't like us.   I swear she don't. So why hang round us and get trips to London?   She's got something on her mind if you ask me."

Gypsy was not ready when they arrived; she never was. "Hurry up, Gyp," shouted her neighbours crossly. "We ought to have her on a lead like a dog," said Hilary.

However, presently she appeared, patting her hair and rather out of temper.   "Good of you to wait for me," she said sourly, "I know I'm only a poor old theatrical."

"Nonsense," said Brendan, starting the car.

"Oh, it's all right to snub me."

"I was trying to cheer you up."

"Likely, isn't it? Oh, you're deep, Mr. Hamp, deep, deep. I know."

"She's worse than ever today, Dad," whispered Hilary.

"Oh, am I?" called a voice from the back.

"Really quite mad," said Hilary, loudly this time.

"Oh, am I? Only a mad old theatrical, aren't I? In that case I feel mad enough to ask if you will give me and Sister Cresta a lift back tonight?" Unexpectedly her voice was nervous.

"Cresta?" repeated Brendan doubtfully.

"Cresta!" said Hilary. "Well we can certainly bring *her*. I shall look forward to meeting her. I was beginning to wonder if she existed."

"Well, I'm ever so glad." And Gypsy leaned back and prepared to get on with her solitary rehearsal.

Brendan drove very fast and with a disconcerting air of not quite attending to where they were going. Gypsy, singing lustily in the back, took no notice, but Hilary found it alarming.

"Don't drive as if I wasn't here, Dad," she complained.

"Sorry," he said, speeding on. They passed very close to an overhanging tree and the branches tore at Hilary's hair.

"Dad!" she complained.

"I've said I'm sorry."

"You didn't even notice what you were doing. Dad," she said impulsively, "I can see you are worried. I know your life isn't all that much fun. You've got Ruth, but I'm older than Jean. I see more than you think about Ruth. I remember more than you think about Mother. I know you cannot forget . . ."

"Shut up," he shouted.

53

Behind them the voice in the back sang determinedly on. Gypsy, having gone through what she could manage of Wagner, was starting on Richard Strauss.

"Oh damn," said Brendan, "I move my family away to a nice house by the sea and they do nothing but complain."

"I didn't want to move," said Hilary; "I liked it where we were."

Gypsy leaned forward and tapped her on the shoulder. "That was Salome I was singing," she said. "I was good, wasn't I? I'd make a splendid Salome if I ever got the chance, I could do the dance as well. You wouldn't make a bad John the Baptist," she said to Brendan leaning back and wrapping her greatcoat round her. "There's a lot of repressed feeling in you, I can see." And wouldn't I like your head on a charger, said her expression.

Brendan drove on, controlling his violence.

Arriving at the office, Hilary said hasty "Good mornings" to the cleaning woman, her fellow-typist and the old messenger and rushed to the nearest mirror to repair the damages of the journey.

"Living by the sea seems to give you a healthy colour," said Mr. Farley, one of her employers. Mr. Farley himself had a healthy colour and excellent spirits, a good deal of which was rumoured to be due to his enjoyment of whisky. He was a great admirer of Scotland, as well he might be. "Ah, I wish I could get away to the Highlands," he would say each long vacation to his younger and less well-briefed colleagues. "But I'm too hard at it, it's all right for you young lads, all the time in the world, but I doubt if I shall get away long enough to make the journey worth while. Ah, you don't know what the place means to me, it's in my blood, it's in my blood"—as indeed it was and on his breath as well.

"I wonder how much violence aggravates fraud?" said Mr. Todd, the most junior of the chambers, "that is, in the eyes of the jury. Or the judge for that matter; what would it add to the sentence?"

"I don't know," said Mr. Farley, "my clients don't get sentenced. Or not often anyway," he added cautiously.

"I've got a woman (calls herself a housewife, they all do of course), and she tried to get ten pounds out of an old girl who lived next door on some rigmarole or the other and when the old girl wouldn't pay up she gave her a black eye. Or perhaps the old girl gave *her* the black eye, it's not clear."

"You don't seem to know very much about it," said Mr. Farley reprovingly. "After all, she's your client."

"Oh no," said Mr. Todd putting down *The Times*, "no client of mine, just something I read in the newspaper. Ah well, I shall know what she got tomorrow. Like a serial story really."

"Reading newspapers isn't what you're paid by your clients to do," said Mr. Farley breathing severity and whisky.

"Nobody *does* pay me," said Mr. Todd mildly. "I don't complain, I understand the system but I'm just pointing it out." He went back to his newspaper. "They say that about five million pounds' worth of diamonds have been smuggled from South Africa this year already. Interesting, isn't it?"

"If you're thinking of adding to the number I shouldn't. You'd surely get caught."

Mr. Todd looked cross.

"I'm only going by the effect you have on judges,"

observed Farley. "You're not subtle, Todd. We can all see you coming a mile off."

Hilary typed on, giving Mr. Todd a sympathetic glance. He was much the nicest of her employers. If she were ever in court, which Heaven forbid, she would certainly *not* want Mr. Todd to defend her; even Hilary knew enough to recognise the disastrous effect he could have on judge or jury, but if it was a question of having her hand held (and she firmly withdrew her hand from Mr. Farley's paw) then she preferred young Mr. Todd any day. However, he never did hold her hand, an occasional look and an air of wonder were all that she ever got from him.

Mr. Todd sat dreaming over his *Times* about fraud and smuggling and large-scale larceny. The subject of smuggling particularly absorbed him. "Big profits," he mused. "Quick returns and no tax payable. Nasty, of course, but do we care for that? No, we don't." And he cut out a piece from *The Times* to add to a collection of newspaper cuttings that he already possessed.

At intervals throughout the day Hilary considered the evening's meeting with Cresta Cresset. In between extracts from *Elektra, Adriadne* and *Rosenkavalier,* Gypsy had brought out that they would be required to meet Cresta at Victoria. Why couldn't the prosperous Cresta afford her own car down? thought Hilary. There certainly was something rum about the Cresset sisters. Hope she likes our luxurious car, thought Hilary with a grin. All the same, she wondered why her father, usually not at all obliging about that sort of thing, had agreed to do it. Brendan was another puzzle these days. He was abstracted, irritable and occasionally violent. Perhaps it was Poll. Hilary herself found her aunt endlessly amusing but she could see that not everyone would share this feeling. She wondered if Ruth's appearance in his life made it easier or more difficult for Brendan to forget those things in the past which he would like to forget. She was certain that his present state was connected with what had happened so many years ago now; unlike Jean, she remembered her childhood.

"That's twice I've asked you if the post was in," commented Mr. Todd. "I'm not counting but I thought I'd tell you."

"Oh, I'm sorry."

"You were miles away. Thinking about Bow-on-Sea, no doubt?"

"If I was thinking about anything I was thinking about Cresta Cresset."

"My dream girl," said Mr. Todd. "Or was when I was at school. Getting on a bit, isn't she?"

"I've never met her. Tea's here, Mr. Todd, will you take yours? Biscuit?"

"Practical girl, aren't you? Go on about Cresta."

"She lives next door to us in Bow-on-Sea. That is, she does when she's home which I don't imagine she is very often, and her sister asked if we could bring them both back today in our car. We bring Gypsy up practically every day."

"Gypsy's the sister?"

"She's Cresta's elder sister. She sings too. You should hear her."

"I'm interested in Cresta. Can I come along too? I'd love to meet her."

"Oh no, Mr. Todd, I don't think you'd better."

"Pour me another cup of tea, Miss Hamp, and give me

another digestive biscuit. I'm going to look up the Cressets in *Who's Who*."

It was no surprise to Hilary that Mr. Todd should be waiting for her at the end of the day or that he should firmly accompany her to Victoria Station where she was to meet her father and Gypsy. One of the qualities which most annoyed the judges with whom Mr. Todd had occasional business was the persistence with which he put his often mistaken point of view. "I know my own mind," he used to say and successive judges had been forced to know it too.

"Here's the bus," he said, putting a hand under Hilary's elbow. "Jump!" Hilary jumped. "Let's go upstairs, you can see more. Evening, Charlie," he said, raising a hand. He turned to Hilary. "That was Charlie, the old messenger. Must be going our way."

"Thought it was him," said Hilary. "Poor old thing. Seems a pity to work at his age."

"We retired him once," said Mr. Todd. "On a pension, of course, then we found that he was around just as much as before he retired if not more, so we took him back again. Worth his while to stay, no doubt," he added thoughtfully. "Up to something and can't afford to be away from it."

"What—that nice old man!"

Todd shrugged. "Plenty going on our way, you know. He's got some little racket all right and it's based on our office. Wish I could find out what it was."

"You wouldn't give him away?"

"Give him away? I'd join him. He's old, in a few years I'd inherit."

Hilary looked at him doubtfully. She never knew

when Mr. Todd was being serious or not, and of this too the judges complained.

The bus stopped at Victoria and Charlie nipped off and disappeared into the crowd. Mr. Todd watched him. "Like to know where he's gone," he said.

The small yellow car drove into the station yard and Hilary saw that it contained Gypsy and her father.

"There they are," she said without pleasure. "In the yellow car."

"That's never Cresta," exclaimed Mr. Todd, "wearing that mustard-coloured dress?"

"Is that a dress?" asked Hilary. "I'm glad you recognise it, I've never been quite sure. No, that's Gypsy, the sister I told you about."

"There's a family resemblance to Cresta all right. Well, well, I hope this meeting isn't going to be disillusioning for me." But he sounded excited.

Gypsy cast an anxious look all round and rushed off to meet her sister, muttering something under her breath.

"Just like the White Rabbit, poor thing," said Mr. Todd kindly.

Brendan raised his eyebrows inquiringly.

"This is Mr. Todd," said Hilary.

"I'm her boss," said Mr. Todd with an agreeable smile.

"Not the one I met before," said Brendan—and not one I want to meet again, his expression implied.

"You're going to have a time with all that luggage," said Mr. Todd watching a porter gradually assemble a pile of luggage beside the yellow car.

"Oh goodness, that's not all Cresta's," said Gypsy, staggering up carrying a great fur coat and a big handbag, "not all that great pile, that's a lot of other people's. Cresta's is only the big black trunk and the smaller cream one just by it and the cream train case to match. And, let me see, that pigskin bag must be hers and the set of check-coloured suitcases; treat those *very* carefully; that's all except for the little hold-all. Not much, you see."

"No, not much," said Brendan.

"She has been round the world," said Gypsy defensively, still staggering under the fur coat.

"That's a nice little bit of mink," commented Mr. Todd.

"*Le vison,*" said Gypsy, nursing the coat and Cresta's big crocodile handbag.

"Yes, that's one that didn't get away," agreed Mr. Todd admiringly.

"What's keeping Cresta?" said Gypsy, glancing at him nervously, her cheeks quite pale with the strain of her load. She wouldn't trust anyone else with them though.

"I don't think this luggage is safe," said Hilary when it was all loaded. The luggage towered above her, the back seat of the yellow car was almost entirely filled with bags and so was the ancient rack at the back.

"I don't think it's legal," said Brendan. "The police'll stop me before we've left London."

"Oh no," said Gypsy with a slight scream.

"Oh yes," said Brendan grimly.

Brendan and Gypsy waited and Hilary and Mr. Todd waited. No Cresta Cresset appeared. Gypsy went off and presently returned with the incoherent statement that Cresta had "Gone another way"—to avoid the Press and photographers, said Gypsy.

Brendan was angry. "Do you mean that we've come here and stood about and waited for her and she's not coming with us after all?" He was inclined to shout.

Gypsy muttered something about it not being her

fault, but she looked very worried. Mr. Todd thought that she looked sick with anxiety.

"Let's go now, shall we?" she said, looking round her.

"Can't be too soon for me," grumbled Brendan. He got into the car.

Out of the corner of his eye Todd saw his old friend Charlie getting on a southward-bound bus in a hurry. "Dear old soul," thought Todd. It was his impression, but only his impression, that there had been a conversation between Charlie and Gypsy as Gypsy had sped off to find her sister. Why had Cresta Cresset "gone home another way"? Not, he felt sure, to avoid the photographers. She wasn't a girl to hide her light under a bushel. But because she wanted to avoid whoever was there to meet her, came the answer from his ready mind.

He looked towards the little group that had assembled to meet Cresta. There was Brendan, Hilary, Gypsy and, of course, old Charlie. They seemed harmless enough.

He noticed then that there was a good deal of dark blue in the coloured picture of the station yard spread out before him. Surely there was an unusually large number of policemen on duty?

He looked at Gypsy and thought that she had noticed this too. "Well well," he said to himself, "so the Cressets don't like the police."

The yellow car set off. It was piled high with the Cresset luggage, and it even contained Mr. Todd. Brendan was angry, Hilary was indifferent and he himself was enjoying every minute. Only Gypsy was both frightened and worried and Mr. Todd thought he knew why.

As they slowed down to pass one of the policemen, Todd leaned out. "Lot of you chaps about today, isn't there? After someone?"

"Just routine, sir," said the constable. "The Soviet Mission is arriving tonight and we don't want no trouble." He waved them on.

A pang of disappointment passed through Mr. Todd. So there was a normal reason for the police after all and they had nothing to do with the disappearing Cresta. Then he saw that Gypsy was lying back with an idiot grin of relief on her face. She had relaxed completely.

"So she and her sister *did* think the welcoming committee was out for Cresta," said Todd to himself. He leaned forward to Gypsy and spoke to her. "Of course the police don't always tell the real truth about who and what they are waiting for," he said, and watched her stiffen up with fear again.

It hadn't been a good day at Bow-on-Sea either.

Ruth and Poll had their first near quarrel and Poll departed in a huff. Ish Murphy had something on his mind and kept making telephone calls and doing calculations. Stephen and Miss Perlott both had letters from abroad which gave them food for thought. And Jean was at school full of brooding anger.

Stephen studied the letter from his father. Sometimes Mr. Bent's letters began "My dear Stephen", but this left some element of unclarity about their relationship—it could have been addressed to someone who was no relation and therefore it was not much favoured by Mr. Bent. Today he began:

My dear Son,
By the time this letter reaches you I shall have enjoyed another birthday, my fiftieth, and I confidently expect that I shall have received a letter from you congratulating me. I

use the words congratulate and enjoy with intent. My life so far has been agreeable and profitable; I am a rich man, my boy, and a happy one. I had always intended that this should be so. Intention however is nothing and execution everything. You might remember that. For instance, I have no doubt, as I have said, that I will receive a letter from you for my birthday; equally I have no doubt that the letter will not arrive until after my birthday, and that the present (surely there will be a present: I always send you one) will arrive even later. Quite likely too the present will be inadequate. You see what I mean? Your intentions are excellent—how terrible it would be if I doubted that—but your execution is poor. You will have to do better. You are clever enough. As my son it was not inevitable that you should be clever, for cleverness, like wealth, is not necessarily handed on, although stupidity unfortunately often appears to be, but at any rate your intelligence was to be expected.

> *Best wishes from your affectionate father,*
> *John Bent.*

Dotty old thing, muttered Stephen. He took in the implied threat and assessed its cause and value.

Mr. Bent had also written to Miss Perlott.

Dear Miss Perlott, he began, carefully claiming no possession for he was a cautious man and was risking nothing, whatever Miss Perlott felt about it:

Dear Miss Perlott,

Here is your cheque for the month's expenses. Please send a receipt (stamped) as usual. Who are the family that have taken the house next door? Tell me more about the daughters. Stephen does not mention them. I find this significant. He constantly mentions Mrs. Hamp and someone called Poll who is not, it seems, a parrot. I wonder what I should read into this? Does it even matter? But I fancy it does. Young men do not always know their own minds. We older people, you agree, Miss Perlott, usually do. I have always felt happy that you and I understood each other. You have been in my household for some years now; it would be a sad pity if we were to be without you. But this would come about through no fault of mine.

I am fascinated by the state of the household bills. If they had gone up I should have been sympathetic, had they remained at the same level as before I should have praised, but as they have gone down I am puzzled. My dear Miss Perlott, can it be that you are stingy?

He remained her employer, John Bent.

This letter too contained something of a threat but so obliquely was it worded that Miss Perlott whose forty-five years—sometimes she looked more and sometimes she looked less—had taught her neither sharpness (except of a kind) nor sense, did not notice it but fancied instead that she saw an invitation. She had had this fancy before.

Miss Perlott probably answered this letter at once and posted it a little later. She wrote other letters too, perhaps too many.

"It's a pity that they taught this bird to write," was how Sergeant Mitchell of Bow-on-Sea City Police C.I.D. put it. He sat down comfortably on his wooden chair with a soft cushion tied on to it. He and his superior shared a small but exceedingly smart and modern office decorated in what they had been told was the "contemporary" style. It was famous in its way and Sergeant Mitchell and Inspector Gibbon had once been photographed working in it and looking awkward for a "Glorious Homes" article.

"She can certainly scratch with her little claw," agreed the inspector. "And draw blood too."

They were in a good position to know, for Miss Perlott wrote to them frequently and complainingly. She complained about the morals and behaviour of all her neighbours, about the noise and drunkenness and laziness of all the workmen she saw at work in the neighbourhood, and she complained about the police. Miss Perlott's letters had so often begun with the phrase that she was "politely requesting" the police to take action that the letters were known as Perlott's Invitations or Perlott's Party. But as she lived near Mariners' Market she found plenty to complain about and altogether the letters were getting less and less gracious and more and more peremptory and generally taking on more the air of a subpoena than an invitation.

Lately she had made insinuations about Stephen's friend Ish Murphy—the Irish labourer—as she called him and also about the police. "How can a policeman afford a Jaguar car?" she ended up.

"How indeed?" asked Inspector Gibbon. "But who does?"

"Maybe she confuses a Jaguar with a Riley," said the sergeant carefully.

"Some people might," agreed the inspector.

"And yours is the same sort of grey."

"It's twenty years old," said Gibbon irritably. "Don't be a fool."

The sergeant was silent.

"And I wish she'd lay off Ish Murphy. He's not a bad chap. He can talk about music."

The sergeant looked unconvinced. "Soccer was his big interest, I thought, or so he said to *me*."

For a moment they looked at each other and then Gibbon laughed. "A man of many interests, I can see. Oh well, I suppose we could go up and see what Miss Perlott is getting at."

"Oh, so we're going to take notice of her at last, are we? I wouldn't let her bully you."

"You and Perlott have got something in common," answered his exasperated superior. "You've both got nasty minds. She isn't bullying me. No, she's been throwing accusations and insinuations out ever since I came here, and it's time we stopped her."

He looked down at the latest communication in which the words traffic, monstrous, unnatural, and adamantine chains occurred. "Might not be a bad idea to see Ish too."

"Where does Ish live?" asked the sergeant.

"In the market of course, where else?" And indeed the market was just the sort of place for someone like Ish. It had a happy-go-lucky, get-rich-quick air which just suited him.

As they walked along the market towards Seaman's Rise and Miss Perlott they saw Ish strolling in their direction dressed in his best clothes. Ish, as his mother used often to say to him, was a fine figure of a man with broad shoulders and strong arms; his impressive figure was well known in the market and heads turned to watch him pass and hands waved to him. Ish responded absently.

"There he is," said the inspector. "Quite a sight, isn't he?" He waved.

"Hallo, Gibbie." On his way towards them Ish stopped at a banana stall and casually selected a fruit. He frowned. "These bananas aren't ripe," he said to
66

the owner of the stall. "I know, Ish," said the man regretfully. Ish ate the banana rapidly, still walking on, and then he threw the skin neatly in the gutter at the inspector's feet.

Gibbon and Mitchell watched his progress towards them.

"Got the royal manner all right, hasn't he?" said Mitchell. "Quite the little crown prince."

Ish listened to what they had to say to him without interrupting.

"I don't know what the old trout's got against me," he said indifferently. "I dare say I do a dozen illegal things a day without knowing it. What do you expect from an Irishman?"

"If you've ever been nearer Ireland than Liverpool I'll eat my hat."

"Oh, I dare say. No, I don't know what she's got against me, but I know what's made her angry. Last time I saw her coming round with that collecting box of hers (the Old Cats' Home it was this time, always something different) I told her that the Town Council were raising the wall at the bottom of Seaman's Rise to stop her snooping over it."

"And why are they raising it?" asked the inspector curiously.

"No idea, dare say they don't know themselves. Maybe the reason why we've got such a lot of bricks round this year is that Mr. Mason the Mayor is owner of the Lime Brick Company. Anyway, I can't bother with Miss Betty Perlott, I've got an old friend coming down to Bow-on-Sea today."

"Can't exactly see you with a childhood friend, Ish."

"Oh, we weren't *children* together, dear," said Ish; "we

67

met when I was a Bevan boy. Did I tell you about that? Before I went I thought it'd be like in the books, hard work all right, but afterwards a good emotional life with women and lots of drink. Dramatic, see? Well, all the miners I ever met worked hard all right but all they ever wanted to do afterwards was to have a wash and take their greyhounds for a walk. It wasn't cheerful, you know."

Gibbon looked at him half amused, half sceptical. Could you ever believe Ish?

"Ah, here she comes," said Ish.

Brendan's yellow car came shakily through the market.

"At least I think that's her among the piles of luggage." He went forward. "Cresta, my old Cosy Corner Sweet."

"She didn't come," cried Gypsy leaning forward from the piles of luggage. "There's no one here but me."

Ish stood back disconcerted. The yellow car swayed on.

"See you later, Ish," said Gibbon. "Mitchell, you can go back. I'll get on to Miss Perlott by myself."

He came to the gate of the Bents' house just as the car with Brendan, Gypsy, Hilary and Mr. Todd stopped too.

Ruth and Stephen were standing there side by side.

"Well, what is it?" called Brendan, suddenly gripped with fear.

"It's Miss Perlott," said Stephen. "I'm afraid she's dead."

CHAPTER FIVE

THE FRONT door of Grey Place, the Bents' house, stood open and all the lights were on, an extravagance that Miss Perlott would never have tolerated while she lived.

"Where is she?" said Brendan, shuffling into the house and looking old. "Pull yourself together, boy." This was his way of saying not that Stephen had gone to pieces but that he had better not. Stephen looked at him resentfully but Brendan went on ahead unnoticing; for no tangible reason he was very much afraid.

"Where is she? Come on, don't be afraid. I've seen lots of dead men." Which was true, but never a dead woman—except one.

Stephen led the way to the kitchen. He paused at the door. "I think she must have just done the washing-up and then started to make herself a cup of tea or something; the kettle's boiled dry and burnt, it's that you can smell, and that was why I came in, otherwise I should probably have gone straight upstairs. I'm frightened of fire." He was talking rapidly and nervously.

He opened the door. At this moment Poll came running up. "I told you to wait for me. She needs a woman here now, poor thing, whatever she was like."

"She doesn't need you or anyone else any more," said Brendan as he looked down at Miss Perlott, but if his words were sombre his tone oddly enough was more cheerful. "Yes, it was that last cup of tea that did for her."

"Brendan, what a way to put it," protested Poll as she knelt beside the dead woman. Miss Perlott lay on the floor, her hair dishevelled and her apron untidy; her topcoat lay on the back of one of the chairs where she must have put it after coming in from shopping or whatever she had been doing. "She must have been going to make a cup of tea after doing the sink, you can see she's been cleaning it, there's the cloth and the cleaning powder—I suppose the whole thing was too much for her. I must say you'd never have thought her heart was *that* bad."

"Yes, it was bad," said Stephen, "I do know that."

"Anything can do it if you've a really tricky heart," said Brendan, sitting down on one of the chairs and putting his arms over the back of it. "Just conked out. We'd better carry her up to bed. Stephen, you call the doctor."

"Doctor?"

"Yes, doctor, even if she is dead you don't start with the undertaker, you know." Brendan was brisk. Stephen went out without a word.

"Really, Brendan, you're being pretty hard on that boy," said Poll. "Try to put things more gently."

"I'm being better than gently, I'm being good for him."

"Yes, I know your ideas about being good for someone—kick them in the teeth and then tell them that false teeth are better anyway. I can remember you being good to me like the time you . . ."

"Your friend Bert Gibbon is here," said Brendan with some malice.

"Bert! What are you doing in the corner like that? Why didn't you say something?"

70

"You two didn't leave me anything to say," observed Gibbon.

"The police are supposed to take charge," said Poll, still flustered.

"Nothing to take charge of here. I hope."

Brendan grunted. There was not a strong flow of sympathy between himself and Inspector Gibbon. Stephen came quietly back into the room.

"Of course I know what a nuisance Miss Perlott was to you," continued Poll brightly. "You'll be quite glad to see her dead."

"That's the way to endear yourself to a policeman," said Brendan. "Keep it up." He got to his feet again —he had an idea that he'd better not go too far with Poll, she was not so calm as she looked. "Well, we'd better carry her upstairs and put her on the bed."

"Well, it's not a job I'm going to volunteer for," said Poll. "And don't ask that poor boy."

"He's been in the army, hasn't he?"

"Look at him, he's quite white."

And indeed Stephen was growing pale under the flow of ready Hamp practicalities. He looked at Poll in amazement, she certainly wasn't what she looked, there she was so pretty and little and neat, apparently, and yet so tough underneath.

"I don't know what Dad's going to say," he muttered.

"Can't very well blame Miss Perlott, can he?" asked Brendan. "Is that a car? It's the doctor. You go, Bert."

Gibbon returned with a little fat man with a bag.

"Got the police here already, have you?" said the doctor conversationally, taking off his coat and folding it neatly over a chair. "Who found her?"

71

"I did," said Stephen.

"Moved her at all?"

Stephen shook his head.

"Just where she fell, eh? Cautious, weren't you? Bad colour, poor old girl. Not been dead long." He took a limp hand and let it drop. Then he ran light fingers over her head and down her neck. "Well, I should guess she had a heart attack and died. She certainly had a heart condition although I would have expected her to hang on a bit longer. Still, in my opinion"—he paused and they waited—"very many people *are* in the state where they might drop dead any minute." His eyes ranged over them reflectively, pausing particularly on the inspector, or so Gibbon felt. "They don't know it of course; most of us have got some mortal disease just waiting round the corner for them. Ask any pathologist whether post-mortems on natural deaths don't turn up some surprising things. Miracle is how the human body keeps ticking."

"Well, there you are then," said Gibbon.

The doctor gathered his things together. "Can't think why she did come to a natural end," he said surprisingly. "Miracle someone didn't polish her off before."

"You shouldn't say that sort of thing," said Gibbon. He knew Dr. Beecham of old.

"Well, we all know about her letters, don't we? All over the place, you might say. You should have let me read 'em. I could have given a bit of help in dealing with her. These poor old spinsters. Poison pens. Not that hers were anonymous."

Spontaneous combustion was probably the mortal disease hanging over the Doc, thought Gibbon; he'd just go up in smoke.

72

"What letters were those?" asked Brendan.

"Miss Perlott sometimes made complaints to us by letter," said Gibbon. "About residents in the neighbourhood."

"Complaints!" said Dr. Beecham. "First prize for understatements. Ever mention me, did she?" went on the irrepressible doctor voicing all their thoughts, but the inspector ignored him.

Silently Miss Perlott made the journey up to her bedroom. It was a large room with two windows, one facing across the garden and towards the sea and the other looking out on the road, a window much favoured by Miss Perlott for her observations. By this window stood her writing-table; it had originally been her dressing-table but as Miss Perlott took very little pains with her dressing and much with her writing she had made a conversion. It was a big mahogany table neatly piled with Miss Perlott's papers, pencils and pens, her little notebooks and her big blotter. Her anxious and heavy pencil had scored vindictive tracks across the good surface of the wood. There were no pictures in Miss Perlott's room; her employer had offered her a picture of his latest mining project but this she had refused. But she had plenty of useful little mirrors in her room. In spite of its good proportions and handsome furniture it was an ill-favoured room and had absorbed much of its user's personality.

The bearers placed Miss Perlott on the bed. Poll, who was hovering outside the door (she had kept her eyes shut all the way up), now came forward. "Hadn't we better put something over her? Be more decent, wouldn't it?" Unlike Poll to ask so many questions, she usually knew the answer right away to all things but she was certainly nervous.

"Stop fussing round, Poll," said Brendan who was equally nervous. "It's stuffy in here. Oughtn't we to open a window?"

"Miss Perlott never opened windows," said Stephen; "I don't know why, one of her things; I wouldn't like to do it now."

"You'd better come back with us, Stephen," suggested Poll. Her eyes were on the inspector who was moving alertly round the room. He had no official standing, none at all, but it did occur to him while he was here that he would like to see if Miss Perlott had had anything to go on, any evidence, and had kept it, of the multitude of accusations she had at one time made.

"You could open a window for a little while, then close it," he said absently. He went over to the big window and lowered it for a second. From the dip below the hill where the market lay he could hear noises.

"Still beating it up in the market," he said with a frown.

From outside there was a loud whistle and then the hissing of a rocket in flight. Fireworks too!

"What is it?" asked Poll.

"It started with a sort of party, so I gather from the doctor, for the banana-stall man." The inspector frowned. "At least, I'm not quite sure if it was for him or whether he was giving it. He was dancing 'Knees up, Mother Brown' and Ish was leading the band."

"Dreadful place," said Poll primly.

"The market isn't so bad," said the inspector tolerantly. "It's got its standard, you mustn't judge it like other places. Think of it as more like Africa, primitive, a jungle."

"Listen." Brendan held up his hand. "They're not playing 'Knees up, Mother Brown' now."

74

"Harsh sophisticated sound, Ish's gramophone," said the inspector.

"*The Rite of Spring*," said Brendan. "What is this? An initiation ceremony?"

The jungle drum went on beating away. Loud laughter and the sound of fireworks, another rocket!

The inspector closed the window. He looked down at the figure on the bed. He was unable to resist, even though it had been demonstrated to him that it was none of his business, trying to reconstruct her last minutes alive, trying to make out what sort of a woman she was. Her face was little and lined and the mouth pouted; the look of quick shrewd intelligence had not left the face with death, a hard face but not a stupid one. It was impossible not to believe that this person had had some truth in her many accusations. How much perhaps the inspector would never know. Unless she had kept a diary, but he looked again at the face and knew that that closed-in, shut-up face was not the face of a woman who had ever kept a diary; her face and her room were closed up.

As he looked at the room he noticed that every drawer and cupboard was closed, and every surface bare, no hairbrush or cosmetic on the dressing-table, no pictures or books on the bed-table; only on the writing-table was there any trace of the life of the woman who had lived in the room for so many years now. And even on the writing-table the pad and the blotter were bare.

"Was the room always like this?"

"I don't know," answered Stephen, "I never was in here much. And do you think we could go out now? I'm not really enjoying this conversation in here, just now."

"Well, I will just cover her up," said Poll fussing forward. "Poor thing, it wouldn't be right . . ."

She brushed against the wardrobe door which swung open. The cupboard was almost empty, at the back not even on hangers but simply hung up upon pegs were the few clothes Miss Perlott was accustomed to wear every day—the old grey tweed skirt, the blue woollen dress, the red jersey coat and skirt were all well known to the Hamps and to Stephen—but hanging in the front of the wardrobe, well separated on silk hangers, was a complete and new set of clothes, silk dress, coat, hat and shoes. They were brightly coloured and obviously expensive; underneath, folded on clean tissue-paper, were light underclothes and a small fur stole.

"Lord," said Poll. "Lord."

Gibbon came over and had a look. "Never been worn."

"She hasn't had them long," said Poll. "That style of collar only came out this spring, absolutely up to the minute."

"But are they hers?" asked Brendan.

Gibbon looked at Stephen who shrugged, and then he turned to Poll and raised his eyebrows in question.

"They're her size," said Poll. "Yes, I should say they were hers for what my opinion is worth. They're expensive and new, but not really good style; they're the sort of things someone who didn't know would buy."

Gibbon was fingering the fur stole; as he picked it up he uncovered a little cardboard box; for a moment he hesitated, then he opened it.

"Make-up," said Poll. "Well, who'd have thought it? She was going gay."

"Is it her colour?" asked the inspector in what he thought was a knowledgeable way.

"How can I tell?" answered Poll impatiently. "She might have been going to change her colour, in her place I certainly would have done. You can do anything with make-up.

"I suppose I ought to tidy the room a bit," she went on, picking up a scarf from the floor. "Not that it needs it. I might shut the window."

She walked over to the window and leaned across the shelf full of bleachers and cleaners to close the window. "Never saw so many disinfectants and cleaning powders in my life. Do you think she used the lot together? She was pathological, poor thing. Do you know Ruth told me she never washed up without using a bleach to whiten the things too? Something funny there all right. Not that she made a very good job of the sink, poor old thing, must have been feeling funny even then." A strange look came over her face. "Bert," she said, "you know what I think about all the clothes and things in this room? Something borrowed, something blue, something old and something new—old Perlott was going to get married."

"Or thought she was," said Gibbon slowly. "Or thought she was."

Poll decided that they really couldn't leave Stephen alone in Grey Place and that he must come with them. They locked the house and then stood for a minute irresolute on the doorstep with a chill wind nipping at them.

"Well, I expect it's a weight off your mind that she's gone and all," said Poll to Gibbon with an air of saying something to cheer everyone up.

The inspector drew in his breath. "I take my work seriously of course," he said, "but I try to preserve a certain detachment too. Good night, Poll, night, Brendan, night, Mr. Hamp."

He departed.

"You never can keep your mouth shut," said Brendan to his sister. "As the inspector himself would say, don't *say* that sort of thing."

"I was only trying to be cheerful."

"Of course you were," said Brendan. "It'll be the death of you yet."

By the time they returned Mr. Todd was firmly established in the Hamp household. Ruth had invited him to spend the night.

"Is everything all right?" said Ruth, raising inquiring eyes. "I thought we'd better not all come crowding over. And there was nothing we could do."

"Stephen's staying with us," announced Poll.

"Shall I, Ruth?" he asked. "I won't if you don't want me to."

"Oh, but of course you must."

As a family the Hamps took Stephen up to his room and showed every sign of lingering, but in the end they departed. Stephen sat on his bed and thought.

There was a knock on the door. Jean put her head round. "I thought you might not be able to sleep so I've brought you some books to read." She offered them diffidently.

"Oh, thank you." Stephen was genuinely grateful.

"I can get you some others if these won't do."

"These will be fine, thank you."

For a moment Jean lingered on the threshold, then she

nodded and went away. Stephen looked down at the books she had brought to him.

He smiled, took up one and lay down on the bed to read.

Brendan had not yet gone to bed. He was shuffling irritably round the house demanding aspirin.

"What do you want aspirin for?" asked Poll. "It won't help you to sleep."

"I don't want it to make me sleep. I don't want to go to sleep. I've got a headache."

"Well, I'm not surprised," said Ruth, producing a bottle of aspirin. "After all you've had to drink."

"All right"—and Brendan took his aspirin. "You two go to bed. You look tired, Ruth."

"Yes, I will I think, it's been a big day what with one thing and another."

She went up to bed and after a pause Poll followed her. She waited for a moment outside Stephen's room wondering whether to go in or not but meeting Ruth's eye, for she too was on the landing, decided not to.

Downstairs Brendan went over to his desk and stood before it thoughtfully. It was an old piece of furniture, perhaps the nicest in the house; it had belonged to his father and was made of rosewood with a delicate inlay. He was proud of it, no one else used it. Nor did Brendan much; somehow you couldn't think of the right words to make a nation-wide appeal about cat meat at a delicate little bit of furniture like that.

From his pocket Brendan drew out a small piece of paper, not writing-paper, but blotting-paper. He had torn it from the corner of Miss Perlott's blotter. On it was lightly pencilled one word. Moira.

Moira had been his first wife's name. For a long time

Brendan sat looking at it in silence and without moving.

Then he opened a drawer and feeling carefully in it drew out a manilla folder. He blew the dust off it for it was not one he had touched for years and took out a glossy double sheet of paper printed in black and white with a touch or two of red. "The Mandalay and Indo-China Rubber Association" it was headed or, as it had jocularly been called, "The Moira Scheme".

It had been a gold brick confidence trick of the simplest and stupidest order, even if Brendan himself, when he so obligingly gave his talents to producing publicity for it, had not grasped this evident fact. Or was this true, had he not always closed his eyes gently, blindly, to what it was so much better never to see; had he not perhaps always known more than he was willing to admit?

It hadn't been a particularly successful fraud, the chief author of it having gone off hurriedly without having ruined more than a few people. Brendan himself had, somehow, escaped the notice of the police. They had never known about him. But now he wondered if perhaps Miss Perlott had not known.

Or if she had not known about the Moira Scheme, she had known about Moira. And Moira, that poor loved lost creature, led back (and how straight back and with what reason only Brendan knew) to the corruptions of Mr. Bennett, the true begetter of the Moira Scheme.

Brendan was thoughtful. He found Miss Perlott an ambiguous character.

He roused himself at the sound of Ruth calling him. He went out to meet her; she was standing at the front door which she had opened.

"Listen . . ."

The noise from the party in the market had died away to a low singing, a curious sort of keening noise.

"Whatever is it?" asked Ruth.

Brendan listened. "What a party," he said.

Mr. Todd rolled himself off the sofa in the sitting-room where he was uncomfortably spending the night. He was not unpleased with the result of his expedition to Bow-on-Sea. He had taken in a good deal and thought it added up to something.

"Party," he said coming over to stand by Brendan. "That's not a party, that's a wake."

CHAPTER SIX

NEXT DAY when the news about Miss Perlott came through to Organ's the undertakers they were working overtime—keeping things under, they said. The shop was tucked away in a corner of the market in a discreet position; there was no sense in bringing forward to the market how transient were its pleasures. Moreover, since most of them were highly uncertain of their status in this world it would not do to remind them that their status in the next was likely to be even more doubtful.

"Ah, I thought we'd have news of her coming in," said the proprietor. "She's had a bad look about her for some time now. All the same, I'd have given her a bit longer. Just goes to show you can't tell."

"You always know, Dad," said his apprentice son admiringly. "You knew about Bill Bottom."

"That was different," said Dad shortly. Bill Bottom had been an inhabitant of the market, well disliked for various tricks which had resulted in the profits of the traders there being severely cut. He had also been a man of much violence with an unsavoury past. He had died in an accident and very suddenly so that Ted Organ's remark was tactless. "Hand me the spirit-level."

Their work-room was at the back of the house and although Mr. Organ was a quiet man and so were his customers, there was a certain amount of noise attached to his work. Ish Murphy who lived next door complained that the noise of the hammers disturbed his sleep. "It's a melancholy thing to be wakened by the sound of coffin nails being hammered in. Many's the time I've leapt from me bed only half awake thinking it was me that was being nailed down."

"Went to a smashing party last night," said Ted by way of conversation.

"Tch, tch!" said Mr. Organ irritably. "How many times have I asked you to keep away from that sort of thing? Ish again, I suppose. I wish you wouldn't. People don't like it, you know."

"Not many of 'em in a position to recognise my face again," said Ted; "we don't usually meet but the once."

The telephone bell rang. Ted rushed to answer it. He was not supposed to receive personal calls at work, but in fact most of the calls were from his girl friends ringing up to see how he was and when he could take them out. Ted, in spite of his father and his unpromising trade, led a full and varied social life which he kept masked from his father as much as possible. A naturally open boy, he had been driven to endless subterfuges by the austerity imposed on him by his father. "Dad lives for his job," he complained moodily to Ish, "but I'm a hearty boy, I am."

He was also a boy ripe for intriguing and this Ish observed, making the resolution that he would enrol this likely candidate for dishonesty. As a result the telephone at Organ's was the channel for many more voices than Ted's girl friends. Perhaps it was just as well that Mr. Organ was growing deaf.

"Ah yes, certainly," said Ted as he put the receiver down. "We're asked to go round to Mr. Bent's house, Grey Place, now."

The two men buttoned themselves into neat dark

83

overcoats and set off down the street. They walked side by side, one tall and fat, the other short and fat, and they walked decorously and in step.

Half-way through the market they met the inspector.

"You've heard the news about Miss Perlott, I dare say?" murmured Mr. Organ in a discreet whisper.

Gibbon nodded.

"It was a surprise," said Mr. Organ wagging his head. "Oh yes, definitely a surprise."

"Oh well, she had a weak heart," said Gibbon. He remembered that Mr. Organ was reputed to know everything that went on in the market and he put to him the question that was on his mind. "Had you heard anything about her getting married?"

"What, married? Her?"

"Any idea who it could have been?"

"I haven't. She wouldn't have been everyone's cup of tea. I shouldn't put too much trust in it myself."

Gibbon nodded. This was the second occasion the mention of a possible marriage for Betty Perlott had been received with scepticism. Sergeant Mitchell had roared with laughter. And yet Gibbon could swear that Poll's guess had truth in it.

Up and down the market on the day's routine business (there was always something in the market that required a little investigation) the inspector inquired as tactfully as he could if anyone had heard a story about Miss Perlott getting married. He could pick up no information at all. Poll was mistaken, he told himself, and what are you bothering about it for, anyway? The old girl died naturally, didn't she?

Then in the photographer's shop he found something. The photographer had had Miss Perlott in there recently.

"Oh yes, she was getting her passport photograph renewed," said the photographer. "Got to get a new passport, she said."

"Out of date, I suppose?"

"Well yes," said the man doubtfully. "*Could* have been that." He paused. "But somehow I had the impression from something she said that it was because she was going to get married."

Ish was outside the photographer's shop staring in at his image reflected in the shop window and patting his hyacinthine curls.

"That's a new hair-do, Ish, isn't it?" asked Gibbon. Ish's hair was round-cropped, spring-curled, not quite a crew cut and not quite like Henry V, although it reminded Gibbon of something.

"Where'd you get the idea from?"

"Pictures, see? Not Hollywood, proper pictures, Roman it was. Quite a lot they were, those old Romans." Ish laughed and stroked his hair. "Quite imperial, isn't it?" And he drew himself up.

"You had a bit of a party, hadn't you?"

Ish was silent. "Just having a bit of fun," he said at last.

"Celebrating something, were you?" asked Gibbon who, like Brendan and Mr. Todd, had formed a certain opinion about the party.

"Now what would we be celebrating?"

This time it was Gibbon who was silent for a few thoughtful minutes. "How did you know she was dead?" he asked finally. "How did you know she was dead?"

"Fidgety Joe spied in and saw her dead," said Ish sullenly.

Gibbon knew Fidgety Joe and believed the story; Joe

85

was an essential part of the efficient if informal information service of the market. He was a little man with excellent eyesight, well-developed hearing and insinuating habits and what he didn't know about the market was . . .

"Ask Joe if he knew anything about her getting married," said Gibbon turning away, "and then you and I can have another talk."

By this time Mr. Organ and Ted had arrived at the door of Grey Place.

No one answered their ring at the door but Mr. Organ bent down and lifted the front door key from underneath the stone—he knew where it was kept, as indeed he knew pretty well everything that went on in the market, deaf or not. Perhaps he knew more than Ted guessed, and it was this that worried Ted.

"It's not right," said Mr. Organ looking up solemnly, "to leave the deceased unattended, not right at all. It's not what's to be considered suitable."

But Miss Perlott was not unattended; in the kitchen sat Mrs. Beckett dreamily drinking a cup of tea.

"Ah, you've come, have you?" she said, but not looking up from her study of the tea-leaves. "I saw it in the cup."

"You might have seen us at the door if you'd seen fit to open it," said Mr. Organ, sharply for him.

"Ah, don't raise your voice in the house of the dead. I knew you'd get in. You always do, don't you?"

"You're not one to trouble yourself, are you?" said Mr. Organ half admiringly. "Well, up we'd better go." And he drew his little face into suitable lines of gravity.

"You take yourself seriously, don't you?" observed Mrs. Beckett, pouring herself out another cup of tea.

"You ought to be glad of it."

86

"I dare say I shall be in my time, but then let's look on the bright side; I might outlive you, mightn't I?"

"I'll just be going upstairs," said Mr. Organ with dignity.

"Give my love to Miss Perlott," said Mrs. Beckett.

Mr. Organ blinked.

"Callous old cow," said Ted when they were very nearly out of hearing. "She's not sorry to see Miss Perlott gone." A shriek of derisive laughter followed him to show that Mrs. Beckett had heard every word.

"Well, don't judge her too hardly. It wasn't nice what Miss Perlott did to her."

"If you ask me it was the one case where Betty Perlott did right. That Miss Biddy Beckett was a mother's girl all right, and look at Mother! Still, I can see old Beckett wouldn't take kindly to having her little dear put away behind high walls, although I'd have called it a blessing. I bet the neighbours did."

"It was the manner of doing it," said Dad, breathing heavily. "I knew more about it than you did—you were in the army."

As they came to the top of the stairs they heard unmistakable sounds of movement.

"What's that?" said Mr. Organ.

He threw open the door and there was Gypsy on her knees looking in Miss Perlott's wardrobe.

"Er—it's a nice time of the year, isn't it?" she said. "I was just saying good-bye to Miss Perlott."

"On the floor?" asked Ted suspiciously. He and Ish knew a bit about Gypsy.

"On my knees," corrected Gypsy with dignity. "Didn't it look like it?"

"Did you find what you were looking for?"

Gypsy ignored him, she got up, and with a sort of bob to the still figure on the bed, went out and down the stairs. They could hear her humming faintly to herself as she went.

"Good-bye," yelled Ted after her.

"Quiet," reproved his father. "You're forgetting yourself again. I don't like the atmosphere here, Ted, 'tisn't right. There's no harm in the old Beckett, but what was that other one doing here?"

"It's the two of them together," said Ted. "Gives you a nasty feeling, although I prefer the old Gypsy to that Beckett woman any day."

"Mind what you say," reproved Mr. Organ, letting his eyes travel slowly round the room taking everything in. He saw the china dishes filled with bits of old string and rubber bands and old stamps; he saw the carefully stacked boxes and tins, and layers of brown paper; he saw the neat little bowl of old buttons, broken beads and old jewellery. Kept everything, he thought.

"She was no friend to us," said Ted solemnly. "You won't say you're sorry to see her go."

"Tch, Ted"—and Dad scuttled round the room. "Your tongue."

"And don't say it'll be the death of me for I couldn't bear it."

But Mr. Organ was not listening, pensively he was rubbing his spectacles and his little face was growing longer and longer.

Far away in the distance could be heard the sound of Gypsy, still singing.

"She's pepped up, hasn't she?" observed Ted. "Quite hep, isn't she? Miss Perlott wasn't so fond of her either, whatever she says now." He paused. "Hark at her, gay as a lark. Not that a lark ever made that sort of a noise; she's really grooving along, isn't she?"

"I don't know where you pick up that sort of language," said Dad irritably.

Screams of childish laughter were added to Gypsy's voice.

"Listen," said Ted gleefully. "Even the kids seem more cheerful now old Perlott has gone."

"Yes, she was no friend to little children," said Dad.

"She was a friend to little soldiers though," said Ted with a snigger.

"What do you mean?"

"Oh, you're still listening, are you? But you know the answer to that one. She was always hanging around the Boys in the Cosy Corner Café—lending a hand was what she called it, voluntary work. It was free all right, but I can tell you that what the boys called it was . . ."

"Don't say it," said Dad with an involuntary look towards the bed. "But what's the Cosy Corner Café," he added suspiciously. "I've never heard of it. Not one in the market, is there?"

"Cosy Corner Café, N.A.A.F.I., rhyming slang, you are slow. That old Gypsy knows all right"—and once again Ted gave his unlovely laugh.

"I don't know where you pick up this language," grumbled his father picking up his tape measure. "You never hear me using it."

"I pick it up at my jazz club, that's where, it's very smart, and if *you* used it, Dad, I wouldn't."

He was watching his father closely all the time and now he drew close to him and the two men looked at each other in silence, then Dad drew away and began to fidget round the room. Ted watched him for a little while.

Downstairs Mrs. Beckett sat quietly waiting by her teapot. She heard the interchange with Gypsy, and afterwards she heard the soft tread of their feet and the creak of the boards, then there was silence.

She sat for a while enjoying her thoughts, but the silence puzzled her. Used as she was to Mr. Organ's ritual she was accustomed to a sequence of little noises to which she could name an appropriate action; dead silence was unusual and even alarming. In the circumstances peculiarly alarming.

"Makes you quite nervous, don't it?" she said aloud to herself. She tried her teapot and found it empty. The kitchen door swung open but there was no one there.

Mrs. Beckett got to her feet.

"You all dead there?" she called up the stairs.

The stairs creaked under Mr. Organ's solemn tread. "No need to make jokes, Mrs. Beckett."

"Joke? I wasn't joking," said Mrs. Beckett with feeling. She poured some more water in the pot.

"No, I won't have a cup of tea, thank you, Mrs. Beckett."

"Well, it is getting a bit weak," she said, giving it a stir, "but then we all are. *You* look weak enough—not ill, are you?"

"I don't like the look of what I see upstairs," said Mr. Organ heavily.

"I dare say not. I don't say I did. Stands to reason, we none of us do. But it's your job, isn't it? You must see a lot of it."

"This is a particular case."

"Well, poor thing, she wasn't no beauty."

"There's something wrong up there," said Dad almost in a whisper. "She didn't die natural."

Mrs. Beckett poured herself a cup of weak tea, sugared it and drank it slowly. "Well, I say you're wrong," she said. "How do you know?"

"I know," said Dad. "That's the sort of thing you get to recognise."

"She had a weak heart and she died," said the sceptic.

"Her hands aren't right," said Mr. Organ. "Her face isn't right . . ."

"Go on."

"And then there's her feet." He put his two plump hands together before him and rested them on his hat. "She had her shoes put on after she died." He looked dramatic. "It all adds up, she didn't die natural."

"Well, you'd better see the doctor," said Mrs. Beckett going to her tea.

"You'd better see the police," said Ted from the door.

"Oh, you're one to talk about the police, you are," said Mrs. Beckett with animosity. "You and your jazz club."

"The police and the jazz club don't quarrel, Mrs. Beckett, they know a good club when they see one."

"Got them in your pocket down there, haven't you? Or is their hand in your pocket? Been wondering myself." She got up. "Well, it's nothing to do with me, but in your position, Mr. Organ, I should think mum's the word. People won't like it if you start calling in the police every time you don't like the look of their dears as are departed."

"Anyone would think, Mrs. Beckett, that you didn't want us to go to anyone at all."

"Oh, it's nothing to do with me. I only want to help you. Where would you be if it wasn't for me?"

"Just where we have been many times—in difficulties."

"I can't help thinking, Mr. Organ, that you're forgetting one thing. You ought to go to Mr. Stephen, this is his house after all. Taking too much on yourself again, Mr. Organ."

Mr. Organ drew himself up. "I know my duty, Mrs. Beckett. You won't make me forget it. Sticks and stones may break my bones, Mrs. B., but words will never hurt me."

"There's some your late wife, my dear friend Mary, called you that hurt you right enough," observed Mrs. Beckett.

"James Organ knows what to do. I don't overlook my respect to Mr. Stephen. I shall speak to him, but I have my own conscience, James Organ has."

"Oh, I know all about that. Consciences run in your family, don't they? Your grandpa confessed his sins so much at the Sankey and Moody meetings that they wouldn't let him into them at the finish. You could see their point too, hardly decent they were by the finish, him having a fine imagination and no sense, and even revivalists have their standards. Mr. Organ, they said to him in the end, we're glad to hear you're a brother saved by the Lamb but would you mind confessing privately in future, and all the time your grandpa was groaning 'It's me conscience, me conscience', and words tumbling out of his mouth. Not that *I* understood them, I was only a little 'un."

Ted gave a short laugh.

Mr. Organ buttoned himself into his coat. "Come on, Ted, we must be off."

"'Bye, Mrs. Beckett," said Ted, "see you again, no doubt."

"Was that all true?" he asked as they walked.

"Some of it, I dare say, but the worst of it is that she's

such an old liar you can never be sure. She'd swear it was gospel."

"Will you go to see the doctor?"

"I don't know what to do, Ted; she was right about Mr. Stephen, but where is he? And I don't want to hurt his feelings if there's nothing wrong. It's not nice, Ted, and he's a nice boy, one of these sensitive ones."

"Like me," said Ted.

Dr. Beecham's house was at the end of the market, a tiny red-brick Georgian cottage.

"There's the doctor in his garden now."

The doctor was wandering round his garden with a little red notebook which he consulted at intervals. "Two tulips gone today, and another red hyacinth. 'Morning, Organ. They've been at my flowers again, blasted thieves! My God, they've had plenty today, some of my best, hardly worth growing flowers here for people to pinch. Lot of thieves you are in the market."

"Why don't you try growing cacti, doctor," said Ted leaning over the gate.

"Not working for you, Organ?" asked the cross little man.

"I'm an undertaker, not a florist, Dr. Beecham," replied Mr. Organ.

"I meant your son."

"He is, Dr. Beecham."

"Curious, I could have sworn I'd seen that face around with Ish Murphy."

"We've come round on business," said Ted hastily.

Dr. Beecham raised his eyebrows. "Well, go on. My business is your business, eh, Organ?"

Nervously Mr. Organ told Dr. Beecham what he had on his mind. The doctor looked serious.

"I'd say you were making a fuss about nothing," he said. "My judgment stands. She had a heart attack, she had it coming and it came."

"But why did it come then?" persisted the undertaker.

Dr. Beecham shrugged. "Act of God, you know, we can't find a reason for everything that happens."

Mr. Organ still looked worried.

"Oh, you're a man of tender conscience I know," said the doctor. "Runs in your family, doesn't it. I've heard about your grandfather who gave up butchery because it was against his principles to kill."

"It isn't true," said Mr. Organ driven to anger. "He was a respectable ironmonger who gave it up because screws were fluctuating and he wanted a steadier trade. I've heard enough stories about my poor old grandpa, and they all start with Mrs. Beckett."

Meanwhile Mrs. Beckett, having stood for a moment in thought, put on her coat and hat, locked the door as a precaution, then crept upstairs to Miss Perlott's room. Quietly and thoroughly, yet neatly, leaving no trace, she inspected the body.

She looked at the feet. "He may be right about the feet, although I don't see how he can tell."

She looked closely at the face and noticed the slight reddening of the skin around the eyes and nostrils. "Wonder if she'd been crying? But who would she cry over?"

She studied the hands and saw the rough red skin. "She might have been having a fight," said Mrs. Beckett thoughtfully. "Yes, I reckon that's it, she'd been having a fight." She covered up the body thoughtfully. "Now whoever could she have had a fight with?"

CHAPTER SEVEN

IT WAS pretty Aunt Poll advancing gaily into the market, minding her own business, and hoping everyone was doing the same, who put the next foot into trouble. She didn't realise quite what she was doing or even Poll would have drawn back.

"Now, my pretty Poll," Brendan had said to her only that day, as he got ready, very late, to drive to London, "keep that tongue of yours quiet and your little hands in your own pie."

"As if I wouldn't. Honestly, Brendan!"

"Good-bye, Ruth," said Brendan ignoring Poll. "I don't need to tell *you* to mind your own business as you never do anything else, but don't eat too many cakes, will you, girl. That's your particular sin of the flesh."

"I thought you loved every inch of her," said Hilary as she pulled on her best white summer gloves. She was also wearing her new hat.

"So I do, but I'm not insatiable."

"Don't mind me," protested Ruth, "I just love to hear you talking as if I wasn't here."

"It's Mr. Todd who doesn't seem to be here," said Hilary with a worried look. "What did you do to him last night, Father?"

"He'll be about. You get in the car, Hilary. I don't believe you're so sweet-tempered today."

"Well, it certainly is time we left, it's nearly three o'clock. Hardly worth going at all, I should think."

95

The Hamp family had risen late and angrily and sleepily disinclined for work. Even Jean had failed to go to school.

"I'm dreadfully hungry," she said plaintively, "but all you do is talk about food."

"I hate to tell you what Freud thought was the reason for overeating," said Hilary who certainly did seem to be in a bad temper.

"Oh, she's a growing girl," said Ruth giving her a pat.

"Not any longer, I hope," said Poll waspishly. "Look at her now, she's enormous. Don't you want to make yourself attractive to young men, Jean? And how she can eat after last night I can't think. It gave me a shock I can tell you."

There was a silence. So far there had been a curious reluctance to speak about Miss Perlott. Now Poll had dragged it into the open.

"Oh, her," said Jean with a shrug. "We're better off without *her*. I can't say the thought of her being dead's any trouble to me."

"You really can be a nasty girl, Jean," said her aunt. "I've really got quite a headache this morning. But I expect that was the noise your father and Mr. Todd made last night, staying up drinking."

Brendan stood up; he felt like the general in charge of a disorderly army, an army that didn't yet know that it had a battle to fight. He looked round at them despairingly, *he* knew that there was an enemy about.

"Aren't I taking Todd to London? Where is he?"

Ruth put a gentle hand on his arm. "That silent presence in the back of the car is Mr. Todd. He doesn't feel so good this morning."

"Good Lord, is that a man? I thought it was a bit of Cresta's luggage that got left over."

"What were you and he drinking last night?"

"Slivovitz."

"And what's slivovitz?"

"Comes from Yugoslavia. Made from plums."

"Oh, like jam."

"No, *not* like jam." Brendan smiled with some satisfaction. "Well, apparently it was too much for Mr. Todd."

Mr. Todd eased himself carefully into the room and sat down.

"Oh, there you are," said Hilary with pleasure.

"Yes," said Mr. Todd, "here I am. Or so I believe. But I think you'd better check with your father. I'm not sure, this morning, if I'm not a case of mistaken identity. Or a split personality at the very least. My head I'm sure doesn't belong to me and it's certainly splitting."

"I shouldn't trust old Todd very far if I were you," said Brendan, settling back comfortably. "He's been to Russia. It all came out last night."

"I was only eight," observed Mr. Todd. "My father was out there working."

"What's it like there?" asked Poll curiously.

"Oh, conditions there aren't as bad as you'd think. It's murder in the towns of course, eight people in a room pretty well, but everyone who's anyone has their little country house—dachas, they're called. And damned uncomfortable little huts they are too," he added thoughtfully; "hardly any sanitation or running water."

"I shouldn't have thought a boy of eight would notice that," said Poll suspiciously.

"Ah, I hadn't been away to public school then, you

know," said Mr. Todd mildly, "so I still had fairly high standards of comfort."

When they had departed Poll and Ruth sat and looked at each other.

"Where's Stephen?" asked Poll.

"Still asleep."

"Have you had the thought that Jean likes him?"

"Perhaps."

"Be a pity if she does, because he isn't likely to take much notice of her."

"Don't you think so?"

"No, I'd say he was more likely to look for someone older, more sophisticated. Boys like that often do," said Poll carefully.

"I'm worried about Jean though, I'll admit. She's got so dreadfully aggressive lately. I wonder sometimes if she's got a really nice nature."

"Oh yes, she has," said Poll. "All us Hamps have."

"Oh I know, of course. But perhaps she's a less nice Hamp."

"She's always very nice to me."

"Oh yes, and to me as well. She likes us, you see. I just wonder about the people Jean doesn't like."

Poll shrugged. "Oh well."

"Yes, I know, but there was a girl at school that Jean took a scunner to, I never knew why. Well, one day that kid had a bad accident, fell down and broke her leg. Jean wasn't a bit sorry, she was pretty pleased I think."

"Oh well, she's only a baby really."

"She isn't a baby and you know it."

"You don't understand the Hamp ways."

"I married one, didn't I? And, my God, I sometimes wonder why."

"As a matter of fact, dear, so do I."

The two women eyed each other.

"Poll, what really did happen in Canada?" asked Ruth. "I've been longing to know."

Poll looked solemn. "It was a pretty big business," she began; "my husband turned out to be quite different from what I expected. I thought I knew him like a book."

"And didn't you?"

"No, dear, or any rate, if I did, it turned out to be the sort of book I didn't like reading." She paused. "And he was so mean." She paused again considering his meanness, then she went on briskly, "But there was more to it than that."

Ruth saw that no further information was to be given. She sometimes felt with the Hamps that she was acting a part in a play—comedy or melodrama, she never knew which—and that they knew the part and hadn't told her. Anyway, she said to herself with a grin, I've got more than a walking-on part. I wonder if they know that?

In a little while Poll had departed to spread the news of Miss Perlott's sudden death. She found that the news was pretty well distributed already but most people were willing to hear it again. And Poll had details of her own to add. For instance, until she arrived it was not generally known that the police (or one policeman anyway) had been present at Grey Place. "Of course, Inspector Gibbon was there," Poll would say, "naturally"—thus contriving to awake in the ready imaginations of the market the conviction that the inspector had been up to something.

Soon there were rumours and counter-rumours going round the market. "Have you heard the buzz?" a voice would whisper. "Well . . ."

99

Poll went trotting round, shopping and enjoying herself, with no idea how explosive the situation was.

As she passed the Post Office she paused for a moment. For a moment she stood still enjoying the sunlight, then there was an angry roar which struck her ear-drums, filling them with waves of sound, and a harsh flash of light which pained her eyes. Without realising she had moved she found herself leaning against a wall and screaming.

Deafened, dazzled and frightened, she began to smell burning.

Cresta and Gypsy were on the telephone; they were quarrelling with the false and loving gentleness of sisters.

"I'm *so* glad you've been having such a good time while I've been away," began Cresta, "making such friends."

"Oh, they're not bad people," said Gypsy. "Got some funny ways perhaps, and the girls haven't got very nice manners."

"You'd know about that."

"But Brendan and Ruth have been very decent."

"Well, I'll tell you something," said Cresta sharply, "I've seen *him* before. Or else it was his picture in the paper. I'll remember soon."

"Oh, I know all about *that*," said Gypsy and she giggled.

"By the way, have you got any money?"

Gypsy was surprised. "Oh, but I thought you'd got . . ."

"I daren't touch that yet, too risky."

"Oh, Cresta, I do hope nothing's gone wrong!"

Gypsy was very nervous now. The trouble was that you couldn't really trust Cresta. "I was always against it, but you argued me over, you said it was almost a duty, so I agreed to help, but . . ."

"Help," said Cresta in a shrill voice. "I take all the risks; you haven't done a single thing except post a few letters and taken a few messages. I did all the dangerous work. And it was dangerous. You should have seen those men in Cape Town. I thought, if they put their hands on me I shall scream."

"And did they?"

"Well—not in violence, at least not really, they were just very strong men. Stupid though; still they were awfully sun-tanned so it didn't seem to matter. Of course the climate out there is wonderful. The brandy is good too."

"I haven't got any money," said Gypsy, anxious to settle that point.

"Oh, there'll be plenty soon for everyone can't you—see that?" asked Cresta impatiently.

What Gypsy could see in her too suggestible imagination was one of two alternatives, either a cold, if rich, grave, or else a tiny cell in a women's prison, for that they would get caught somehow was her deepest conviction.

"You must get hold of Ish," said Cresta urgently.

There was a flash of light across Gypsy's eyes and a low grumble of sound. She screamed.

"Something terrible's happening here."

In London Brendan was getting on with the plan that had been his real purpose in going to the city that day. It looked as though Miss Perlott had known about the

Moira Scheme; well, so unfortunately had a lot of other people, including the office of the Public Prosecutor. But Miss Perlott had called it the *Moira* Scheme and that nickname had been restricted to three people: Brendan himself, his wife who was dead and Mr. Bennett, the originator of the whole nasty business who was possibly still alive but had disappeared.

Brendan turned down the Strand and into a narrow side street. It was about eighteen years since he had come this way last, and war and bombs had come in between. The shops had changed and Brendan hesitated once or twice in an uncertain way. But the junk shop was unchanged; it had turned itself into a "Wireless and spare parts" shop but its general appearance and, it seemed, its stock, remained the same. With renewed confidence Brendan opened the door.

A man was sitting at the counter turning over a grubby book. He was wearing a thick tweed overcoat and dirty cap pulled low over his ears, a woollen scarf was swathed round his neck and drawn up like a burnous. He moved his head cautiously and Brendan looked at what could be seen of his face.

The shop had changed hands.

"It's the weather," said the man. "In great pain I am. This weather always brings on my neuritis."

Brendan studied him doubtfully, perhaps it *was* the old proprietor, changed by the years and neuritis. After all he had only come here once or twice in the past, once with Mr. Bennett and once with Moira.

"I've come for the box you were keeping," he said at last, producing the old formula. "Name of Holder."

There was a moment's silence.

"Do you mean you're Holder?" asked the man, "or

the box is in the name of the holder? If so, what is it?"

"Oh, just give me the box," said Brendan impatiently. "You must know if you've got one or not. Never mind about the name."

He was sure by now that whether this was his old acquaintance or not the man was a party to too many illegal tricks to be treated gently.

"Holder's the name," he repeated.

"That isn't magic, you know." The man was wiping his nose, one cloudy grey blue eye alertly studying Brendan. "Holder now you say, well, there might be a box and there might not."

"You've changed since I saw you last," said Brendan.

"You never did see me last," said the man, not ceasing in blowing his nose.

"I'm not so sure," said Brendan bitterly. "Your face has changed but your manners haven't."

"Ah, they go with the job, stock-in-trade."

"Yes, you've got more stock here than you display," said Brendan, looking round the shop at broken chairs, old sofas, piles of old books and bits of brass. "What about that box? Diamonds in the aspidistra, eh?"

The man's eyes moved.

"Ho! Diamonds is *passé* these days. We 'ave things better than diamonds."

"Diamonds are never *passé*," said Brendan with conviction.

"You don't look like a diamonds man," said the shopkeeper appraisingly.

"No. I had other interests."

"Ah. Well, you don't look as if you did very well by them. 'Had' you said?"

"What about that box?" said Brendan.

The shopkeeper sat down heavily on his chair and nodded his head towards the back of the shop.

"You know where to look, Holder," was all he said.

"In the old days," said Brendan, "you went and got it."

"In the old days," said the man, "that is if there were any old days, I couldn't have been in my right mind. What, stick my neck out for the cops to twist it? If there are any boxes I don't know where they are and I never touched 'em. Look for yourself—if you *are* Holder, which I doubt."

Brendan pushed past the counter, knocking over a row of old vases.

"Don't knock the stock about or I shall have to charge you."

At the back of the counter was muddle and dirt. Brendan shivered. Everyone has something in their past that they are ashamed of, he supposed. His was perhaps rather special. He could make nothing of the confusion he saw. The trouble was that he had no idea what the box for Holder was like or where to find it. He had only been here twice and on each occasion he had been too sunk in embarrassment to take clear details in. Or so he supposed.

Nothing like a row of boxes was to be seen. How many clients had in the past kept their uneasy secrets in this repository? How many boxes, how many crimes?

He looked thoughtfully at the rows of pots and bottles and old biscuit tins. "Everything here but the kitchen sink," he said to himself and then he saw that tucked away in the corner the sink was there too. Unused, of course, the shopkeeper was an unwashed character.

Uneasily he moved up and down the lines of old furniture. He could see a row of cardboard boxes behind a stack of chairs. Boxes were boxes but somehow these did not seem the right boxes; he opened one to see an old hat and a nest of mice. It struck him that Holder's box had better be well fastened down or it would have been eaten up long ago. A depressed helplessness replaced his earlier determination and he sat down.

"Cold," said the shopkeeper. "All cold."

Behind the shopman stretched a long mirror which looked as though it might have come out of a Victorian bar, and underneath the mirror was a long shelf laden with earthenware preserving jars, each carefully labelled and sealed. Brendan looked at them again. Memories of what Holder's box had really been began to seep back into his mind.

The man saw him looking. "Everything that's got a lid's a box, isn't it?" he jeered. "Go on, Holder, pick out yours."

"When is a box not a box?" said Brendan crazily to himself. And answered, "When it's a jar!" He picked up one of the large preserving jars. It was labelled "B".

In the jar was a roll of neatly folded documents. Among them he hoped to find something which would help him to know, one way or another, if Miss Perlott had known about or been part of the Moira Scheme.

First to turn up was all that remained of the correspondence between Mr. Bennett and Brendan—all that remained meant that Mr. Bennett had carefully burnt anything that in any way reflected on himself and had equally carefully preserved what incriminated Brendan, and as Brendan had been young and silly and free with his words this was a good deal. The total effect, as perhaps

Mr. Bennett had calculated, was to put the burden of guilt fairly upon Brendan.

Upon my soul, I don't know why the old boy skipped, thought Brendan. If he let the police have these I'd have been in jug and he'd have been over the hills and far away. Couldn't get them to the police perhaps. Not like him to spare me anything. Well, I wonder where he is now? Prospering somewhere, the fat louse.

The few letters that remained of Mr. Bennett were neatly typed.

"My God, there was certainly someone else who knew what there was to know. He never typed these himself."

At the bottom of the page were the initials M.M. And as he saw them a face he had forgotten floated up from his unconscious mind. A thin, scrawny, anxious face. There had been a secretary after all. She had been called Margaret, he thought, and he remembered nothing else about her. She might have been Miss Perlott, she might have been anybody.

Also in the box was a train ticket and reservation, London to Edinburgh, dated September 6th, 1940. One funk ticket had never been taken up. Well, that seat had been filled long ago.

There was one letter in pale blue ink written in a free curling hand that he held for a long moment before he dared to open it. This must have been one of the last things stowed away by old Bennett. Brendan had never seen it before. But he knew the writing. It was the writing of his late wife.

Ten years ago, he told himself, you'd have given your back teeth to have read this. And now you don't want to open it. You're frightened.

Yes, I'm frightened, Brendan said to himself. But good-bye, fear, there can't be anything worse for me to know.

There was only a page of the letter present. It was an extract from the middle of a letter without beginning or end.

> *By the way did I tell you I was wrong about Mums—I call her Mums, she wouldn't like it if she knew—we don't have to worry about her. It's a nuisance the way she's been snooping but there's nothing in it. She won't do anything, I swear it. She* is *like a little bird really, isn't she? Extraordinary, isn't it? And I know some birds can talk as well as sing but she won't. I was as gay as a lark with her. Gay . . .*

and here the page ended.

"Everything's here, I suppose?" he asked.

"Oh yes," said the man, "barring the things I sent through the post."

"Through the post?"

"Special post order," said the man smugly. "*You* know the arrangement. Address at Bow-on-Sea." The man leaned forward. "Nasty time they seem to be having down there. Death and disaster. You wouldn't know, but I got word private, just come through on the blower. It happened this afternoon. . . ."

The telephone rang again from the back of the shop, and when the man returned to pursue the Londoner's favourite sport of making his auditor's flesh creep, the door was swinging in the breeze.

Brendan had gone.

Hilary and Mr. Todd had arrived at Gray's Inn together slightly sheepishly. Mr. Todd was very cheerful and

Hilary slightly remote. Her chill good-bye at the top of the stairs puzzled him; he did not realise that the well-balanced Hilary was off balance for perhaps the first time in her life, and that she found it difficult to adjust herself to what she took to be their new relationship, difficult to get back to the old Mr. Todd–Miss Hamp relationship after the extraordinary events of last night. Not that poor old Perlott's death had been extraordinary. Or had it? Hilary powdered her nose thoughtfully.

Mr. Todd was sitting quietly in his room making an effort to bring himself back to complete consciousness. The old messenger Pickering shuffled into the office.

"Thought this was your day off," said his employer. "Haven't you got a life outside this office?"

"You don't want a day off at my age," said the old man eyeing Todd cautiously. "I'm laying up stores for another world."

"Thinking of being a space man? I bet you've got some reserves salted away in this, though," said Mr. Todd with admiration. "I'm on to you, you know."

"Go on, Mr. Todd"—the old man was unperturbed—"on to what?" He laid a few letters on the table and cleared away the waste-paper basket. "You do like your little joke. Supposing I was to take you seriously? What would happen then?"

"Sudden death, I should think," joked Mr. Todd and then went white. He watched Pickering's retreating back with apprehension. "Silly of me to say that to him. Still, it isn't likely that he carries a little bottle of cyanide round with him just on the chance he might want to knock someone off. But a lot of other things could happen to me, I suppose—a fall downstairs, a little push under the nearest bus, they say there's nothing easier."

He walked across the room and looked over the tree-tops to Chancery Lane and the Public Record Office. "There must be some record somewhere of what's been going on," he told himself. "Somewhere they must have left a trace, nothing would be committed to writing that didn't have to be, of course, but they'd want to see that everyone involved was equally committed. Old Pickering'd be up to that one."

He sat down to think. Hilary appeared with a note-book and a few documents.

"Ever thought of old Charlie Pickering as a dangerous character?" he asked.

"What, that poor old boy? Certainly not, he's as harmless as an old pussy-cat. Mind you, he's not very *nice*."

"Letters," said Mr. Todd thoughtfully. "Really?"

He was beginning to recover his courage. He took out from the large book-case by the window a handsome atlas that his mother had given him for Christmas. He studied first the map of Australasia and the islands of the Pacific. Then he took from a drawer one of his sister's letters, this was the sister who had married an Australian and gone out there to live.

Dear Toddy boy,

Here are the cuttings and odd photographs you asked for. I can't think why you wanted them. I hope you enjoy the account of the Russell Farmer girl's wedding. She looked better than that really. Oh well, perhaps not. Still, she's got fine teeth, you'll admit that, which is just as well in the circumstances.

Mr. Todd's sister's letter then continued with family gossip none of which Mr. Todd bothered to read. He picked up the newspaper cuttings. They seemed to be mostly from the *Sydney Spectator*. There was a gay and chatty article about the marriage of Miss Russell Farmer, "a lively member of our younger set. Welcome to her as a bride, her groom is Mr. Pearly Nikoliodds. He is a dentist". "Not what we used to call him when I knew him," said Mr. Todd who had, as it happened, been at prep. school with the man. "Yellow Dog Dingo *we* called him." After the wedding the guests had been entertained by a cabaret starring the English singer, Cresta Cresset and some of her dancers. As the guests departed each lady was given a small piece of costume jewellery as a present. "The bride's father," said the paper, "had them specially designed in his costume jewellery factory, one of the largest in the country. Each brooch represented a tiny tooth, made of pearls and embraced by the letters P. and R."

"Charming thought," said Mr. Todd, putting the letter and its enclosures down. He opened a drawer and took out a small envelope carrying newspaper cuttings sent to him by yet another sister—they were a far-flung family. These cuttings came from South Africa, from Durban, Johannesburg, and Cape Town papers. They all dealt with entertainments in hotels and theatres and in each the name of Cresta Cresset was prominent. The *Cape Town Courier* actually published an article with the singer. "I've had such a good time," said Cresta, "that I don't want to go home. My girls and I have had the most tremendous success." And there was a photograph of Cresta, looking remarkably like Gypsy, wearing a good deal of the chunky jewellery she had done so much to make famous. The *Johannesburg Echo* was cheerful and vulgar. "Why do the kids stay in Jo-burg?" it asked in flaming capitals. "It's so difficult to get my girls to come home with me," complained Cresta. "I brought out a large band of dancers, and where are they now?"

"Where indeed?" said Mr. Todd to himself. He had been following Cresta's activities in the papers for some time now and had come to certain conclusions. "I bet you've taught them not to go out with the raggle-taggle Gypsies oh!"

He thought it was pretty clear what Cresta, and probably Gypsy, had been up to. And he had a sort of feeling that neighbour Miss Perlott had known too. But she was dead.

Still, it had been a natural death, from heart failure.

Far away in his memory a voice began to speak; the voice was the voice of a doctor friend of Mr. Todd's and the scene was a bar, full of noise and smoke.

"Death from heart failure," the voice was saying sceptically. "*All* deaths are deaths from heart failure—the heart just stops beating—but it's what stops the heart that counts."

Mr. Todd held out his hand to see if it trembled; it did.

"Hope nothing stops my heart," he said to himself. A refrain began to repeat itself in his mind: "I know what's been done but I don't know who's doing it. I know the game, but I don't know the players." And perhaps there are two games, he told himself, remembering some indications of the night before.

Gloomily he took himself out to tea in a restaurant in Chancery Lane where he consumed dry toast and thick dark tea among the hopeful litigants and the even more hopeful students of the Public Record Office.

"You can't trust lawyers," said a loud-voiced little man sitting at the next table. "Wicked they are. Now look what happened to me. Said to me, just tell a simple story, they said, so I did. No one will worry you, they said. Then when I got into court, after keeping me shut up in a little back room for hours and hours, a little chap in a wig gets up and says well, it's very clear what you've told us, Mr. Brown, but are you sure it's what you really saw? Course I'm sure, I said, I've got my eyes, haven't I?" He paused to eat some more before going on with his story:

"'Yes, I see you have, Mr. Brown,' said the little 'un. 'You don't wear spectacles I see, Mr. Brown?'

"'No, of course not,' I say short, 'I've had good eyesight ever since I was a boy.'

"'Ah, but you aren't a boy now, Mr. Brown. How long is it since you had your eyes tested?'

"'I've *never* had 'em tested,' I says. 'I told you, I've never had no trouble with me eyes.'"

He ate some more.

"'Well, with his lordship's permission,' says this old codger, giving a little bow, 'we'll test 'em now. Can you tell me what that is you see at the end of the room?'

"'What,' I says, 'that great red thing like the end of a bus?'"

The witness looked up from his food aggrieved: "Well, how was *I* to know that was the bleeding judge?"

Todd giggled, he knew Mr. Justice Wellbeloved.

"Thought my old codger in the wig would have a fit. 'Oh, my lud,' he says bouncing up and down, 'I beg pardon.' But the judge had the last word, he was a game old card, he leaned forward to me and said to me, 'That'll teach you not to be deceived by appearances, Mr. Brown,' he says."

Don't be deceived by appearances, thought Mr. Todd.

He rushed back to his office. An anxious thought was rumbling round his head like a wasp trying to get out of a jam pot. At his door he met Hilary. He waved her to a chair, ignoring her attempts to talk and reached for the telephone. Eventually he got his number only to have a dim voice say that the doctor was having his tea. There certainly seemed to be a good deal of giggling and movement in the background.

"So I hear," said Todd.

"You can't have, old boy," said a rich voice. "It isn't that sort of tea."

"How would you set about causing death by heart failure?" asked Mr. Todd.

The doctor laughed. "Thinking of doing someone in?"

"No," said Mr. Todd cautiously.

"Well, nature's got various methods," said his friend cheerfully. "You can't really do better than she does, but if you are really cast upon your own resources . . . How's the customer's heart?"

"Weak."

"Oh well, your job's half done for you, isn't it? However, to help things along I should say the methods fall into three general groups. First, have you tried a really good shock? Can't really beat it, but of course you can't make an impression on some people, got hides of leather. Secondly, you get at their respiratory system— like the good old London smog, nature again, you see, but you might work out a variant. And then of course you can force the subject into a good deal of physical exercise, a fight would do it, especially if you could work in a dash of No. 1 as well."

"Thank you," said Mr. Todd.

At that moment he saw old Pickering poke his head round the door.

"Get out," he shouted.

Hilary's mingled feelings stirred into anger.

"I think you're perfectly horrid to that old man," she said. "In fact you're insufferable altogether. Lording it round. Oh yes, I noticed you making fun of poor old Brendan last night. Oh, you think you're wonderful, don't you?"

"Hilary!" Todd's voice was hurt.

"You'd treat me like old Pickering if you could."

"You're thoroughly strung up, and no wonder with all that's going on."

"Going on—what is going on? I don't know. Now tell me to get out like old Pickering. I know you'd like to."

"I'd marry you tomorrow if you'd have me."

"There, that's what I mean. You are insufferable. You think I'm a fool. What a fool you'd look if I said yes."

"Try me."

"Right, I will. What time?"

Mr. Todd was silent.

"Well," he said finally, "I don't know about tomorrow. Let me think."

"Go on."

"I'm appearing before Lord Justice Stinger (and he is my dear) but on Thursday week I've a day free."

"That's right, fit me in between engagements."

"Hilary, you fool." And after a pause: "Will you always be such a shrew?"

The next pause was longer. "What will the other secretaries say?" said Hilary, raising a delighted face.

"That's right, what will they?" said Mr. Todd, alarmed.

"And, oh my goodness, I've never told you what I came in here to tell you."

"Well?"

"I had a telephone call from Ruth. There's been a bomb explosion at Bow and the Post Office has been blown up, and," said Hilary racing on, "somehow Poll's mixed up in it."

Todd looked at her and all his fears flooded back.

Only Brendan knew nothing about the explosion as he raced the yellow car home to Bow-on-Sea—he had taken the old junk shopkeeper's words to mean Miss Perlott's death. He drove fast, even faster than he usually allowed himself, finding some relief in the speed.

He stopped for petrol at a garage about ten miles away from Bow-on-Sea. The place was empty except for a couple of cyclists drinking lemonade and listening to their portable wireless, and a young man dressed in a pale lemon jersey and suède shoes. He got up from the piles of tiles he was resting on and supplied Brendan with his petrol and then sat down again to polish his nails.

"Do I need some oil?" asked Brendan, all his irritation returning.

"I couldn't say," replied the young man, "but I'll get one of the boys." And he strolled off.

Brendan sat in his car and waited. He waited with growing impatience and then he got up and banged at a bell which said "Service".

"He won't come back," said one of the cyclists kindly. "He always says that when he's bored." He bent down to touch the car. "Nice old car you've got here. No need to look at me like that. You are an old doubting Tom. I'm telling you what is so."

"Thank you," said Brendan savagely and drove off. He did not like the look of either of the cyclists.

In the mirror behind him he could see that the two cyclists were following him.

Except for him and the cyclists the road was deserted. He drove absently, his thoughts on what he had learnt from the old junk shop.

The ambiguous figure of Miss Perlott revolved in his speculations.

The cyclists drew level and then passed him. As if on a prearranged signal four more cyclists appeared on the road ahead of him. They were coming towards him slowly. He slowed down himself, waiting for them to divide and let him through.

But they did not divide, they came steadily on, strung out in a line across the road.

He would have either to stop or run through them.

If he stopped, then he was alone in the dusk with a group of unknown young men. He began to have a dim idea of what might happen to him if he slowed down.

He hesitated for a moment more, staring at the swaying figures. Then the strain of violence, which was in Brendan and which had twice in his life before almost wrecked him, rose to the surface and he accelerated and drove straight at them.

CHAPTER EIGHT

THE MARKET was used to being blown up, it had been blown up three times in the memory of the youngest inhabitant—which was not so very young, for the market tended to be a stable community. Death or a prison sentence might remove a few but once a Mariner always a Mariner was to be a true axiom, or as someone once put it, "Once in you daren't get out." The first explosion of contemporary memory had been a real explosion, the sort that kills people, although naturally it hadn't been tactless enough to kill any adult Mariner. "The best thing that ever happened to us," was how the inhabitants viewed the German bomb, as the damages claimed allowed for the rebuilding of the entire market which had badly needed it. The second explosion took the back off the police station and no one really minded about that either except Sergeant Mitchell whose best boots and trilby went up in the blaze and who therefore minded very much indeed. The cause of this explosion was very mysterious but it was publicly stated to be due to a leaking gas main. The last explosion was when Granny Organ blew up with her gas oven and this was generally believed to be the best thing that had ever happened to her, too.

"Due to an explosion in a gas main," was the explanation offered in the stop-press of the Bow-on-Sea evening paper, but this was discredited in the market.

"'Tisn't likely now, is it, when the only gas they use there is when they talk?"

Not even the police believed it was a gas explosion, Inspector Gibbon, Sergeant Mitchell and a large red-faced man toured the area of the explosion. It hadn't. after all, been a very big affair.

"Didn't do much damage," observed the large man.

"Depends what you're used to, I suppose," said Gibbon. The inspector and the bomb expert had taken a quick but deep dislike to each other.

"We'd like to know what could have caused this," said the inspector. The explosion had brought down part of one wall in the back premises of the Post Office and broken a few windows but the main damage had been caused by the short but sharp fire which had followed.

Mr. Madge put on a dark brown cotton coat and proceeded to his inspection. "You'd better step outside," he said. "You can never tell. I prefer to take any risks myself."

"Thanks," said the inspector.

He and Sergeant Mitchell waited restlessly outside while Mr. Madge did his work. Their time was occupied with soothing the anxious inquiries of the Post Office staff—an old lady, a fat girl, and a thin boy with adenoids. As all three lived outside the Mariners' Market they naturally had not the iron nerves of the locals nor their heaven-sent conviction that whatever happened *they* would be all right.

"What's he doing in there?" asked the youth. "We got a right to know. This didn't ought to have happened."

"I can see you've had a nasty shock," said the inspector in what he hoped were soothing tones.

"It was a bit more than that, I can tell you. I was just out there boiling a kettle for a cup of tea . . ."

"Thought you didn't have gas laid on here?"

"It was an *electric* kettle, and then came this rumble and

flash and there I was sitting on the kettle. I might have got a bad burn."

"Yes, and he would have done too," said the girl, who seemed exceptionally stupid. "Only the kettle wasn't hot. Don't look at me like that, Jimmy."

"Still, I expect he got damp," said the inspector who was on her side.

"No need to make fun, we're public figures we are, in the P.O. If we're struck then England's struck, I say. What about the bomb? Did it have enosis written on it?"

"It could have had halitosis written on it for all he cares," said the old lady revealing a strong Scots accent.

"Now don't you start, Mother," said the inspector. "Let's wait until Mr. Madge has told us what he knows."

"Aye and that won't be much, you can tell by his face."

"Well, we're responsible to the public we are," said the young man who seemed a persevering soul. "And a good deal of the Queen's mail has gone up in smoke."

"Yes, you'd better let me have the details," said Gibbon slowly. He motioned to Mitchell to take notes.

The loss of mail had been substantial. In the market Post Office, which was not, in spite of the pretensions of the young assistant, a very large one, there were two busy periods; the first was just before ten-thirty in the morning when the overnight mail was finally cleared, and just before four in the afternoon when all the morning collection had come in and been assembled. It was this that had gone up in smoke.

At this moment Mr. Madge came back to them. He dusted his hands.

"Quite a little blaze in there." But he refused to say anything more until he and the inspector were alone.

"It wasn't really so much an explosion as a fire."

"What do you mean?" asked Gibbon suspiciously. "Seemed like an explosion to me."

"There was an explosion first," said Mr. Madge, "but it was a small one and I think it was so arranged to set off a fire. It was fixed all right." And he looked worried.

The market received the details of the fire and explosion with equanimity and in spite of the best efforts of Mr. Madge and the inspector to maintain discretion they soon knew all there was to know.

"Ah, it's a good thing it wasn't the day we post our pools," was the general comment. "Now *that* would have been something."

The truth was that they were absorbed in other speculations. And as Inspector Gibbon proceeded on his business about the market he became uneasily aware what these speculations were.

Poll, in discussing Miss Perlott's death, had somehow convinced the market that her death at this moment was a good thing for the inspector, and her screams for Bert at the moment of the explosion had convinced the willing imaginations of the Mariners that Bert Gibbon knew a bit too much about this too.

Exasperated by the double burden Gibbon hunted Ish down and demanded the whereabouts of Fidgety Joe in the hope that he might pry some information out of that slippery character. Joe got his name from the itch in his fingers to pick up all objects of value that came his way. He was tolerated in the market because, owing to his ways, he was a great source of information and the market, owing to *its* ways, usually found it easy to recover any property Joe had got away with. Any that it could not regain it lost philosophically on the ground that Joe must live. The police, too, had found Joe's information useful in the past.

But this time Ish shrugged his shoulders and denied all knowledge of Joe.

"He's over the hills and far away," he said.

So the inquiry to Ish bore no fruit except a bitter reflection that Ish was up to something.

Moodily he made his way round to see the doctor who had examined Miss Perlott.

"He's gone," said his housekeeper who was obviously a close relation of Mrs. Beckett's. "Gone away. Had to. I'd have done the same in the circumstances."

"What's happened?"

"Dr. Beecham was treating old Mrs. Castle for rheumatism in the head, heat treatment, plugged it in the wrong hole, short circuit, blew up."

"Is she dead then?" Gibbon was horrified.

"No no, she ain't dead. Couldn't kill her like that. Better than ever she was. That's the trouble. Brought her powers of speech back and her daughter said that the only thing that had made her bearable was not being able to speak."

In the end the inspector telephoned the police doctor to meet him at Mr. Organ's. He put his problem to the doctor. He had no reason to believe that Miss Perlott had died other than naturally but he was troubled.

"Not the first time I've had to repair some damage of old Dr. Beecham," said the police doctor.

"He's never actually killed anyone, has he?"

"Oh, he's had his little accidents," said the doctor, adding tolerantly, "Still, we all have."

He examined Miss Perlott carefully. He took up her hands and examined them, and then he went methodically over the whole body, breathing heavily while he did so. Gibbon watched him, frowning.

"Seems all right," said the doctor straightening

himself. "Superficially, that is. But I can't tell much without a post-mortem."

"I've no grounds to ask for that," admitted Gibbon.

The doctor took Organ aside and had a muttered conversation with him. Then he returned and examined the face of the dead woman again.

"Nostrils and tissues of the face slightly inflamed," he pointed out to Gibbon.

"Well?"

"Mr. Organ tells me he noticed her eyes were slightly puffy."

There was another pause.

"She might have been crying," said the doctor reluctantly.

So Gibbon sat down and wrote a careful and worried report to his immediate superior on the explosion and also on the death of Miss Perlott.

As a result of the report a few days later a thin gloomy figure got off the London train and complained to the porter about the dirt of the train, to the guard about its unpunctuality and to the ticket-collector about the price of the fare, and set off towards the market.

Superintendent Winter (he had received promotion as a result of the Bartholomew Row murders) had arrived to take over.

He cast a sharp eye over the district as he walked.

"There they are," he told himself, "all getting on with their lives as if nothing had happened. They don't know that I've come to take over."

He was wrong however. The word of his arrival had gone round the market with the speed of light. The whole place had the news and had turned out to watch the superintendent.

CHAPTER NINE

UP TO NOW violence had circled all round the Hamp family, but it had not touched them. Now it was to reach to their very heart.

Brendan sombrely inspecting the front of his car for blood and damage, was hailed by the gay voice of his daughter Hilary.

"Dad, I'm engaged."

"I know that," said Brendan irritably. "What's new about that?"

"*I'm* new," said a modest voice. It was Mr. Todd.

When the situation had been explained to him Brendan did not noticeably cheer up. "A wedding," he groaned. "All I need now to make my day is a bomb."

"We've already had that," said Hilary. "Didn't you notice the Post Office as you came past? Blown up, well, anyway, a bit of it. Bert Gibbon's down there investigating."

"That'll be a help."

"And everyone thinks it's him really, poor Bert," said Hilary with a giggle. "On account of Poll being so cryptic. Poll's very upset now she knows."

Poll confirmed this. "I'm ever so upset," she said. "I wouldn't have done this for worlds."

"All you had to do was to keep quiet, Poll. I warned you."

"I don't suppose Bert will ever forgive me. I don't suppose he'll ever come here again."

"I don't suppose he will," agreed Brendan with his first approach to cheerfulness.

"Except on business," said Poll.

Brendan scowled. "Don't you go producing any. This family will make some soon enough." He didn't know how soon. He went back to his inspection of the mudguards. Seemed clean enough. He hoped *this* wouldn't be the business that brought Bert round.

"Anyway, we've got Hill's wedding to look forward to," said Poll. "That will be nice. They're going to have it quite soon, you know." She paused. "How many people shall we ask?"

"As few as possible."

"I don't call that a nice attitude at all. Your own daughter's wedding too."

"Not for you to talk, Poll. As far as I know there wasn't a soul at your wedding."

"Oh well," she said by way of excuse, "there was a war on."

"*Which* war, Poll? You forget I've got a good memory for dates."

"Oh well, there's always a war on, isn't there?" asked Poll comfortably. "And we must give Hilary a lovely wedding."

"Hallo, Brendan," said Ruth coming forward and giving him a kiss. "Heard the news? Our madhouse is rocking on as usual."

The whole family gathered in the sitting-room where Jean was obstinately continuing to write an essay.

"What's the subject?" asked Brendan.

"Harmony."

"Well, you certainly ought to have some views on that as a member of this family."

"Someone pour some strong drink into Dad," said Hilary, "till he's fit to live with."

"Yes do," said Brendan. "Nasty about that explosion. Hope they discover what caused it. Not what we came to Bow for."

"Or who," said Poll.

"I've told you before," said her brother levelly, "of the dangers of that sort of remark. It's the way of putting things you've got."

"Oh well," said Poll, "it wasn't Bert. I'm sorry if I gave the wrong impression. *I've* got my own ideas." She looked challengingly round the room. "After all, perhaps I shouldn't say it, but I'm in Bert's confidence. He does tell me things."

"Why can I see the top of Stephen's head?" said Brendan getting up and carrying his drink to the window. "And why is it wobbling?"

Ruth laughed as she looked out too. "That's Stephen on his new little motor scooter."

"Well, he doesn't look safe."

"He's better at it than you think. I've been helping him. He's only had it a little while, you know."

Stephen saw them and shouted at them to come and help him.

"Starting off is the hardest," he yelled, "but once I'm really going I don't wobble at all."

They all walked out into the garden and watched Stephen, and even Jean deserted her work.

"Here, let me have a go," said Poll and got on, laughing. "See. I'm good."

For about half an hour they amused themselves with the new toy, laughing and pushing like children, taking turns and then helping Stephen to get what he called "more polish" to his performance. Consciously or unconsciously they were enjoying a short release from the stresses and tensions of the last weeks.

The gate and the front door stood open and no one bothered to look in that direction. As Brendan said afterwards, a "whole army could have gone through that front door and we wouldn't have noticed". "Let's go back in now and have a rest," said Brendan. "I'm tired."

"And a drink," said Poll thirstily.

For yet another half an hour they sat quietly on the Italian loggia by the statue and drank and talked. Presently they split up into groups and no one could pretend afterwards that they had noticed exactly where any other person was.

At one point Brendan noticed Gypsy scurrying past. She waved but did not stop.

"Been out all day," said Ruth. "She doesn't fancy being in the house alone, I suppose."

"Oh, ask her over here," said Brendan, relaxed with gin and ready to be genial even to Gypsy.

He got up. "I'll go to the house and telephone her." Slowly he walked into the house. He was quite steady on his feet but not sober all the same.

Gypsy was only too glad to come. "I'll be over at once."

"Come right in," said Brendan still happy. He put down the receiver and slowly made his way upstairs.

At the top of the stairs he paused and then he saw Poll lying at the door of her room with her head broken in and the bronze head from the garden grinning up at him from the floor.

"My God, come here," he shouted. Then he shouted again.

They came crowding into the house and up the stairs. "Don't come any farther," he said. "Someone's done Poll in."

"It can't be Poll," said Hilary nervously, "we've got her with us."

Poll pushed her way through the group. "It's not me, it's someone I've never before in my life." She looked round suspiciously. "What's she been doing poking round in my room?"

"It looked like you, Poll," gasped Brendan. "You can't see properly for blood. I could have sworn it was you. You want to be glad she was poking round of you'd have been a dead Poll. It would have been you this head fell on. Or me perhaps. I told you not to bring it into the house."

"An accident?" cried Ruth as if she could hardly believe it.

"Yes, one of those accidents we seem to keep having."

"But who is she?"

They turned on the light and looked at the face which was small and painted.

"Hello, hello," said a gay voice from the door below. Gypsy came hurriedly up the stairs calling to them from each step.

"What are you staring at?" she said. Then she gave a scream and fainted. She knew the body. It was Cresta Cresset.

Superintendent Winter hurried first, with Gibbon in tow, to the Bow-on-Sea General Hospital where Cresta Cresset lay. Cresta was not dead, she was unconscious, she might never regain consciousness but she was not dead yet. An exceptionally thick skull had saved her. "She always was a lucky girl," Gypsy had said, gulping down her tears.

"Who is she and what was she doing here?" demanded Winter.

"Oh, you know Cresta Cresset. You must have heard of her."

Winter grunted. He wasn't going to admit it.

The press had been full of the affair. "Accident to famous singer," they had said. "Cresta Cresset fights for life."

"What was she doing down here, and more important, what was she doing in this other . . . the Hamp house?"

"She was down visiting her sister. Often did that. Or she was supposed to," corrected Gibbon cautiously. "Why she was in the Hamp house we don't know. Unless she can tell us when she comes round. If she does come round."

Winter considered all he knew of the affair. "I dare say it could have been an accident."

"The bronze head was pretty securely placed," said Gibbon. "But, yes, I suppose she could just have knocked it over on herself. It's difficult."

"Who had any reason for doing away with her? She got any money? Who would get it?"

"I doubt if she's got much money. May have a bit. I suppose the sister would get it."

"Ah yes, the sister, the unsuccessful sister of the famous singer. Yes." Poor old Gypsy's ears were no doubt burning. Years since she had excited so much interest—except in Betty Perlott. "We shall have to find out about the money. If she does die." He looked down at the small pile of belongings which had accompanied Cresta into hospital. "There's a nice fur coat there, even if there isn't any money; mink, isn't it?"

Gibbon shrugged. "They get fur up so well now."

"It's mink." Winter turned over a little heap of personal belongings. A white handbag, a scarf and a great pile of imitation jewellery. "Funny to wear mink in the summer. And she certainly liked a glitter." He turned over the chunky bracelets, thick necklaces and rococo ear-rings. "Carried quite a lot about with her."

"Oh, stage stuff," said Gibbon, "I suppose."

Gypsy who had been watching them came trotting across. "Can I take Cresta's things home now?" She reached out and scooped up the jewellery.

"Yes," said Winter, then: "No, leave it a bit longer, Miss Cresset. We may need to examine your sister's clothing. Of course, I'm assuming this fall was an accident, but if she dies—well, we have to be sure. The clothing might help."

He was puzzled. No reason why he shouldn't just regard the whole thing as an accident, but like all good policemen there were some accidents he just didn't trust. This was one.

Brendan felt the same. He too was at the hospital, pacing anxiously up and down the long entrance hall. He crossed over to Gibbon and Winter.

"Is she going to be all right?" he asked. "Poor girl. Whatever was she doing upstairs? If it hadn't fallen on her it would have fallen on Poll or me. I think it would have been me."

"We don't know yet if she will live or die," said Winter. "It was a bad blow. How did she come to be in your house, Mr. Hamp?"

"I don't know," said Brendan. "That's what I keep asking myself. Why was she there? What was she doing? We didn't know her, I never met her."

"She came for something," said Winter. "We've traced her on the afternoon train, then a taxi to the market, then nothing—till she turns up in your house." He paused. "She may come round and tell us what happened. I hope so; meanwhile we've got to investigate."

The burden of all that was on Brendan's mind pushed him into unwise speech.

"That head was meant to fall on me, I'm sure," he said. "Someone's got it in for me, I'm sure of it." He thought of the cyclists and was convinced of the truth of what he said.

"Maybe," said Gibbon. Winter said nothing although he eyed Brendan with interest. He liked to see a suspect uneasy, whatever the reason.

Mr. Organ bustled past them. He raised his hat. "My son's had a bad accident. One of those hit-and-run drivers." His voice was angry.

"Was he badly hurt?" asked Gibbon.

"He ought to have been, the bike's ruined, but he got away without a scratch."

He must be made of leather, thought Brendan, the blood draining away from his heart. What had young Organ been up to? He knew very well he had not mistaken the threat to himself.

"He'd better let us have the details," said Gibbon. "And we'll try to get the driver."

"He can't remember a thing," said Organ. "Shock."

Very likely, thought Brendan sceptically. "What about the chaps with him," said Brendan aloud; "didn't they see everything?"

"He was alone," said Mr. Organ looking at him blankly. "He was absolutely on his own."

Superintendent Winter looked from Brendan to Mr. Organ with satisfaction; he was delighted, just on general principles of course, to perceive that they both looked uneasy.

CHAPTER TEN

THE STRANDS which led to murder were being gathered in.

Miss Perlott who had started so much was still and quiet, waiting for her funeral, whereas, so rumour said, she had expected a wedding. From Africa Mr. Bent sent fluent letters giving instructions and advice. The gay girl Cresta lay without moving in a hospital bed, a constable sitting by her side. It was still in suspense whether she lived or died. Young Ted Organ gathered up his smashed bicycle and started a war with the insurance company about damages. And from all parts of the globe letters and telegrams from the affectionate but scattered Todds came flooding in; they were delighted but slightly surprised to hear about William's wedding. The excitement about the explosion died down.

The Hamps, in the middle of their wedding preparations, felt that they were certainly going mad.

"Jean, on your way to school (and must you wear that hat, you look quite square) go down to the *pâtisserie* on the corner by the market and ask about the cake, oh, and while you are there you might say we are providing our own silver vase. I think that's best, don't you?" asked Ruth, turning earnestly to Poll.

Poll did not answer, she was too busy thinking out her own orders. "Jean, will you remember to call at the florist—it's hardly out of your way at all—and tell them that I think a pale green orchid after all. Dark green would be fatal."

Jean grunted.

"And if you said what a pity in that voice I think it was unkind," said Poll whose ears were sharp enough. "Jean, why must you look like a sour cat? Anyone would think you weren't glad your sister was getting married."

"I'm not glad—why should I be? I don't wish her any harm, she's never done me any."

"Don't be cynical. You get that out of your books. You may think it's clever but it's not."

"I wasn't trying to be clever," said Jean wearily. "Why should I be? But after all what do we know about Todd?"

"What do you ever know about the person you marry?" said Poll, forgetting her role of critic.

"That's just what I mean," said Jean, banging her hat down even more squarely on her head. Poll thought how much she had grown up lately, and how sadly mature was the bitter twist to her lips. "This family hasn't got such a good record in the marriage market, has it, that it can afford to be cocky? I'm off love and marriage."

"You're too young," began Poll, but the words died away for even to her it was obvious that Jean was not too young. A little smile crossed Jean's lips.

"Too young to vote or be hung," she said oddly enough, "but not too young to marry." She paused and added in a different voice, "What age was father when he married?"

"About twenty, I think," said Poll in a whisper.

"And look what happened to him. No, don't ask me

what I mean. You know. Good-bye, Poll, expect me when you see me."

She crossed the hall to the sound of voices calling:

"Jean, do ask about the flowers for the church when you go to the florist."

"Jean, do call in the church and see about confetti. I won't have me and Todd . . ."

"Jean, call at the tailor's and see if my silk hat . . ."

"Is this a wedding or a carnival?" asked Jean, hitching her coat over her shoulders. "All right, I'll do it— if I remember."

Screams of protest from Ruth and Hilary greeted this heresy, but Poll pinched her lips and said nothing. She was thinking about heredity and remembering the background of violence and deceit which lay in Jean's descent. She looked down at her own hands, they were strong, ugly, capable and blunt, oddly masculine and utterly unlike the rest of Poll's gentle and frivolous appearance. They were hands which knew how to get what they wanted.

Ruth, strolling in at that moment with her arms full of the white silk of Hilary's dress, saw her looking at her hands, and looked herself. "Cut yourself, dear? Funny hands you've got. Not a bit like you really."

"How do you know what I'm like?" asked Poll as if she was puzzled.

"Oh, the way you look and the way you act."

"That's no guide," said Poll, still studying those hands. She gave a little shudder and then forced a smile. "Sorry to go on like this. It's Jean started it. I'm worried about that girl."

Ruth put on a look of sympathy. " Well, it's difficult for her, Hill's wedding coming like this. She's fond of

Hilary and a bit jealous of Todd, I think. And then there's Stephen—she ought to put that behind her," said Ruth firmly. "He isn't a bit interested in her. Never will be."

"I don't know," said Poll. "God help them both."

"I thought you might know," said Ruth giving her a straight look. "You being in both their confidence."

The two women stared at each other across the white silk dress.

"Not so much as all that," said Poll drawing back.

Hilary appeared at the door and threw her hands up in dismay.

"Ruth, I've discovered that I have nothing *old*."

"Oh, I think we can soon manage that, dear," said Ruth absently. "Now what is worrying me is have we got enough forks? Now did I remember to ask Jean to do something about them?"

"Yes," said Brendan. "Judging from the way I heard you calling out to her as she left I should say you did ask. If not, it was a rare oversight."

"It's good for her to have her mind taken off things," said Ruth defensively. "And you'd be better off at work than fussing around here."

Brendan, torn with anxieties which he would hardly name even to himself, had distracted himself (and the rest of the family aslo) by drawing up a complicated time-table of arrangements for what he called—a little satirically—The Day. Everything had to be according to protocol, he had consulted several books of reference, and had put in days of work on the *Tatler:* the result was a formidable programme typed each day by a complaining Hilary who couldn't see why she should do carbon copies of her own wedding.

"I wish you wouldn't *arrange* everything quite so much," she said irritably, her mind on her own problems. Would an old handkerchief do? "I think a piece of jewellery would be best," she decided. "An antique piece and then it would be old and not old, if you see what I mean."

"And if you make it sapphires it will be your something blue too," suggested Brendan grimly.

"That's a good idea," said Hilary in a surprised tone.

"I wouldn't like you to have anything *cheap*," said her father.

Hilary looked even more surprised. Naturally not, she was thinking.

"Now do you take my right arm or my left when we walk up the aisle?" said Brendan, consulting his spare set of papers. The master set were kept permanently (that is when he was not busy altering the arrangements) on his desk. "We really must decide, so I can work out where we stand at the altar and what we do when we get there."

"The clergyman will know, dear," said Ruth soothingly, taking a cigarette.

"You think I'm going to leave this to a stranger?" shouted Brendan.

"Well, it's your own fault if he is," said Ruth, smoking peacefully. "Never saw you in church much."

"I wish I were getting married in a registry office," said Hilary.

"Registrar. For heaven's sake you're not a housemaid."

"It's about what you are, girl, once you're married," said Poll, reverting to type and forgetting the part she had been playing to Jean.

Hilary burst into tears.

135

"Really, all of you," said Ruth placidly, smoking on. But her hand was jumpy too.

When Todd arrived on his visit that evening he found the whole family lined up in the sitting-room. There were banks of flowers stacked up at the end of the room, and baskets of what seemed to be food and cakes were arranged on all the chairs. Brendan was standing at one end of the room with spectacles on and an armful of papers. His family were rounded up in a depressed-looking huddle, like sheep before a bad-tempered collie. Only Hilary herself seemed to be ignoring the proceedings and was painting her nails on a sofa. Occasionally she spoke.

"I won't do it," she said. "It's the *feet*. I never could stand the feet."

"Er, hello," said Todd. No one took any notice.

"It's the feet," said Hilary again.

"You needn't look at the feet," said Todd patiently, or at any rate with what he clearly intended to be patience. "In fact I don't suppose you will."

"I should feel them," said Hilary, "I should feel them in my bones."

Mr. Todd sat down. He had the sort of feeling he was invisible.

"Did I ever tell you about my first wedding?" he said affably. Still no one took any notice.

"It's because of them being such *big* feet," said Hilary assuming an air of patience in her turn.

"At this first wedding," said Todd, "we certainly had feet. I take that for granted but no one noticed them and they were certainly never discussed. I doubt if they were ever considered, except perhaps on the part of the ushers who had a good deal of walking to do."

"Oh well, if you want your father to go to prison, say so and have done with it," said Brendan explosively.

"I doubt if she really does," said Todd.

At once everyone turned round to stare at him. He was present at last.

"What's it all about?" he said hastily before they lost him again.

"The police. Winter says in view of all that's happened, etc. etc., he must ask me to let there be a constable on duty at the church and at the reception," said Brendan. "It'd look bad to refuse," he added coldly; "Hilary is being hysterical about it."

"Well, I don't know that I care for it myself," said Todd.

"Didn't have it at your first wedding, eh?" said Brendan even more coldly, thus showing that he at any rate had heard every word Todd had spoken.

"You said you'd been married before," exclaimed Poll as if she had just heard the words.

There was a moment's silence.

"He hasn't been," said Jean with decision. "He just happens to have a poor sense of humour." She glared at Todd. "He's making it all up."

"Not quite all," said Todd politely. "Not my wedding. An aunt. I was only six. I was a page." One day the battle with Jean would have to be fought out but not yet. He had the disturbing conviction, known to him before only from detective stories, that a vital piece of information had been conveyed to him, but for the life of him he could not put his finger on it. "Must be all in your unconscious, Todd, my boy," he told himself, "if you aren't making it all up."

"How you can think of marrying him I can't imagine,"

said Jean, going from strength to strength. "He could be married fifty times over for all you know."

"Here, draw it mild," protested Todd. "I'm a slow starter. You can trust me—I've not been married before."

"I don't trust you," said Brendan in a gentle voice, gathering his papers together, "but you have not been married before. I had my inquiries made."

"Oh, you did, did you?" Todd looked at his father-in-law to be with frank interest.

Brendan was silent. One of the advantages of a semi-criminal past was that you knew how to check up on people. Once it had been important to him to know what people you could trust and what people you couldn't. His contacts had not entirely deserted him. He had been able to check up on Todd.

"I can tell you where you went to school and what sort of marks you got. I can even tell you something of your army career. And that I gather was high secret."

"You have been thorough."

"Well, we didn't know anything about you."

"Hilary had been working for me. Don't you take anything on trust?"

"Not any longer." Brendan got his papers together. "As you are here we might as well run through the arrangements again."

Hilary, who had been making up her face with bright pink lipstick, said, "Oh, not again, Dad, I really don't think I could."

However, she found herself back on the couch, with the added advantage that Todd was sitting by her side, listening to her father. "Can't think what's come over Dad," she murmured. "Thinks he's the Pope or something."

Todd winced, "Not really the Pope, dear, you can't mean that. I can see I shall have to look after your general education."

Hilary nodded, "Dad always says I was badly educated."

"By the way, I didn't notice *you* taking much interest in all the talk about me and whether I'd been married before. I was quite hurt."

Hilary got out her lipstick again. "Silly," she said. "You forget, Lucy Douglas and I have been your secretaries for three years now. We know everything about you, we do your income-tax and your insurance. We *knew* you were not married. It was the first thing we checked up on. Then we tossed up."

"Really," said Todd weakly. "You tossed up?"

"Just for the chance, you know; naturally we didn't go further than that."

"Oh, naturally. And who won?"

"Lucy," said Hilary with a small smile. "But she was always a slow girl."

All this time Brendan's voice had been going on monotonously.

"Stand up, you two," he commanded.

Hilary frowned. "Well, I don't know if I will."

"I should, dear," said Poll pacifically, "or I don't think the parson would marry you. You haven't been listening to what your father has been saying. Go on, dear," she said to Brendan. Beneath her breath she muttered that she'd get this lunatic family through this wedding if they all died in the attempt.

"You're at the altar see, Todd. I don't think we need consider the problem of your hands," said Brendan critically. "Just folded in front will look more dignified.

Not *behind*. Too informal, and not by your sides, don't want to look as if you were going to run a race. You'll have had your hair cut, I suppose?" he said, peering over the papers. "Just thought I'd mention it." Todd grunted. "Now we come to arrival of the bride. That's always a tricky point. Unluckily I shall be with Hilary, you really need me in the church, but it can't be helped." He sounded regretful that he couldn't be in both places at once, "That's why we must plan this carefully now. Arrival of bride—here, look it up in the time-table I've had typed for you, at the foot of the page in red: 'Arrival of bride. Groom steps forward. Takes bride's hand. Kindly word to bride from groom'."

"What do you think I'm going to do?" asked a harassed Todd. "Kick her?"

"If you're not going to be serious," said Brendan, throwing his papers down, "I shan't go on."

The morning of the wedding was hot and clear. Stephen waking early saw signs of movement in the Hamp kitchen.

Jean was there making some coffee. She nodded to Stephen.

"Thought I'd find some coffee here," he said, picking up a piece of bread and chewing it. "Agreeable morning, isn't it? Quite a night of it you had last night. What was Brendan up to?"

"I don't know," said Jean, measuring coffee carefully. "I should say he was trying to see how far he could drive us. Well, I hope he knows."

"Yes, you were in a state. However, Hilary was quiet enough. You didn't have any trouble there."

Jean groaned. "That's what you think. Why do you suppose I'm up this early? She's walking up and down waving her hands and crying and saying she can't get married."

"Why not?"

"Says she's in love with Basil Briggs and she's only just realised it."

"But is she?"

"Hasn't seen him for three years," said Jean wearily, "so I don't think she can be."

"No, it don't seem likely. Still, you can't tell"—and Stephen thoughtfully stirred his coffee. "Tell her you happen to know that he's married already."

"In her present mood I doubt very much if that would stop her," said Jean as she prepared to take some coffee up to the bride.

Left alone Stephen sat back to enjoy his coffee. The kitchen was neat and tidy in spite of the flowers and food and glasses and bottles piled everywhere. Only where Jean had been working at the sink was it untidy, and she seemed to have soap powder over everything. Stephen mopped up the flakes and restored the carton under the sink next to the bottles of detergent, Pino disinfectant, and Vigor cleaning powder. "One good turn deserves another," he said to himself making all tidy and then going back to finish his coffee. His world was very good this morning.

Jean returned, looking half amused and half angry. "Would you believe it, when I got up there she was showing Ruth the patterns for the chintz she's going to have in her drawing-room. She seemed to think *I* was the one who was mad. I don't know what Ruth did to her—put a spell on her I should think."

"She's wonderful," said Stephen.

"All Hamps are wonderful," said Jean. "At least for today, no matter what we relapse into tomorrow."

"Expecting much of a relapse?"

"Very big indeed," said Jean. She sighed. "Ruth's done a lot for us. Don't think I don't know that, but we remain a not very nice family and I don't think we've helped Ruth much. The reverse really. I expect she's sorry she took Brendan on."

"Well, I would be," said Stephen, "on last night's showing. No, I'm joking. Seriously, all you Hamps have been very decent to me. I'm going now. See you at the wedding. Save me the first dance if there is one."

"Oh, I will," said Jean eagerly.

This was before eight o'clock in the morning; by midday the whole household was well into its third crisis. It was Brendan this time. He was being got into his clothes.

"For heaven's sake dry up, Poll. You couldn't be more emotional if I was going off to battle," said Brendan irritably.

"Well, that's exactly how I feel," sniffed Poll, wiping her eyes. And indeed Brendan, standing bolt upright and breathing heavily, with his accoutrements laid out precisely all round him, did look remarkably like a Guardsman preparing for battle. His temper was also comparable to someone about to take part in combat— irritable, demanding, anxious and fearful. "You see, Brendan," went on Poll, "you look so handsome. You'd almost think this suit was made for you."

"If that was meant to make me feel at home in the suit it didn't succeed." He put out a demanding hand. "Give me my spats."

"Oh, Brendan, you don't have to wear the spats," said Ruth who looked very nice in flowered silk and a white hat.

"I shall wear everything they sent. If they sent them they must be right."

Ruth shrugged, she was powdering her nose. "Did I tell you Mrs. Beckett asked if she could come to see Hilary married? Nice of her, wasn't it? I said yes, of course."

"She'd come in any case."

Poll put her head on one side. "You know you don't look quite right, Brendan." She had a good look. "I don't know what it is but you look more like a funeral than a wedding somehow." She paused. "I know what it is, it's the hat—they've given you the wrong colour, you've got a black one instead of a grey." She picked up the hat and looked at it. "If you ask me you've got a consignment meant for old Organ by mistake."

At the church Stephen was acting as usher; he had not been as lucky in the draw as Brendan and it was quite clear that his suit had not been made for him. As a result he was constantly tugging the sleeves of the jacket down and the trousers up. It was even doubtful if the jacket and coat had been made for each other. He was being assisted mysteriously by Todd's best man, Mr. Farley.

"Go back," hissed Stephen. "You should be up front, not here at all."

"There's nothing for me to do up there."

"That's not the point, you don't have to do anything. Just stand. And keep Todd from being nervous."

"He isn't nervous, old boy, I am."

Stephen looked at his companion and sniffed the air.

Mr. Farley had clearly been fortifying his nerves with brandy. Almost alone amongst the male members of the wedding he looked extremely dapper and neat but his face was red and his hand unsteady.

"You really must go back, I can see Todd looking for you."

Firmly he took his charge up to the altar. "Tie him up, will you?" he said to the groom.

"Tie him up! He's so full of spirit he'd float like a balloon. I never thought I'd go to the altar accompanied by a smell of brandy."

As he got to the door Stephen looked back and to his horror saw Mr. Farley indomitably tottering (it was an unmistakable totter now) after him. He turned and was immediately engulfed by a crowd of old ladies amongst whom he recognised Mrs. Beckett; beyond them he saw the heads of Ruth and Poll.

By the time he had settled the mysterious old ladies and looked round for Ruth and Poll they were being ushered up the stairs and to the farthest corner of the church by Mr. Farley.

He rescued them and took his three charges up to the altar again. He handed Mr. Farley over.

"Put a pin in him this time, won't you?"

"Who were all the old ladies?" he whispered to Ruth. "Some of them were cheering."

Ruth looked round, "Oh dear, I'm afraid Mrs. Beckett has brought a few friends."

"Few!"

"Well, never mind, they won't come on to the reception—they don't know where it is." And she sat down with the air of one who has washed her hands of the whole affair.

Then Hilary and her father arrived with Jean following morosely behind, looking as she had predicted like a large brussel sprout in her green dress. The organ played and the choir performed wonderfully; a deep baying note in the background indicated that Gypsy had slipped in somehow. The wedding had begun and then was over.

The policeman at the door of the church was really hardly noticeable. The wedding guests departed for the reception. No one noticed that Mr. Farley, quietly drinking whisky in the vestry, had been left behind. No one, that is, except Mrs. Beckett who had every intention of attending the reception too.

A good many minutes later, when Poll was fiercely commanding Jean to hand round the cheese straws, and when Brendan was angrily complaining that he didn't know a soul at the party, and when the bride and bridegroom were beginning to come out of the merciful coma, and the police were beginning to feel that perhaps after all they were out of place, then there was heard the rumble of a large car.

Poll looked out.

A number of old ladies were pouring out of a large car; the car had the door at the back and this puzzled Poll until she saw that Mr. Organ was driving it.

"It's Mrs. Beckett and her pals, arrived in a hearse," she said. "However did they know where to come?"

The old ladies surged triumphantly forward, and in their midst trotted Mr. Farley, gay as a lark and much the better apparently for his long drink of whisky.

"Here we are," he said. "Now enjoy yourself, dears, drinks are on the house, you know."

He rushed forward shaking everyone by the hand,

apparently under the impression he was both bride and bridegroom.

His party retired to the refreshment-table where by sheer onslaught of numbers they succeeded in driving away the rest of the guests.

Todd standing by Hilary's side saw Gypsy and Ish stand together and have one of their underhand conversations. They were never seen openly together but he had noticed they took every opportunity for quiet conversation that was offered. He was willing to guess what they were going to talk about. More, he was willing to listen if he could. Detection at the wedding, well, why not? He had to think of Hilary now.

A large, moist hand fell upon his shoulder.

"Oh, it's you, Farley."

"So 'tis," hiccuped Mr. Farley, now restored to a knowledge of his own identity but drunker than ever. "I want to know why you got married, old boy?"

"Yes, why did you?" said Brendan who was following him up, and who was not in the least drunk.

"The usual reasons," said Todd stiffly. He liked to be the one asking the questions.

"You're a fine father," said Farley to Brendan, "choosing *now* to ask a question like that."

Brendan grunted. He was watching Todd carefully. "I want an answer though." Todd chose his words carefully; he liked to tell the truth if possible.

"I realised that she was a girl who needed looking after. I thought if I didn't get her first someone else might." In spite of himself he shivered. "She might know too much."

The band began to play; it was the Cosy Corner Gang and it played a gay, strangely familiar tune. There was

146

a shout of triumph from the old ladies.   Over the heads of the crowd Todd could see Ish and Gypsy still talking.

"Excuse me," he said, "I can see someone I want to talk to."

He walked off into the crowd.   All round him were old ladies dancing.   Mrs. Beckett, well done in champagne, was leading her friends in "Knees up, Mother Brown".   The dancers slowed up Todd's progress but he continued to push his way through the swaying dancers.

Brendan was also pushing his way with difficulty through the crowd.   He wanted to get to Ruth.   After a while he noticed that someone was trying to get through to *him*.   He stopped and looked.   A white face regarded him over the heads of bobbing singing old ladies.   It was one of the cyclists.   Brendan saw the stiffness of his right arm.   Not here, he thought, not here, not at Hill's wedding.   The man continued to edge his way with steady menace through the crowd.

Brendan stood quite still.   Better get it over.

Then a hand touched him.   It was Inspector Gibbon.

"I'm looking for you and Todd," he said.   "I wonder if you'd mind coming to have a word with the superintendent?"

Relief and anger flooded through Brendan.   Out of the corner of his eye he saw the cyclist halt, and then back away.

"Yes, of course I'd mind," he said, turning round to face Gibbon.   "What's it all about, Bert?"

"Well, Brendan," said Gibbon hesitantly.   "There's quite a story behind it, Brendan, quite a story."

CHAPTER ELEVEN

ALMOST FORTY-EIGHT hours of ceaseless activity lay behind Gibbon's meeting with Brendan Hamp. Superintendent Winter had seen to it that they were hours of hard work for all concerned. The meeting between Inspector Gibbon and his old chief, Superintendent Winter, had been the meeting between two equal and slightly hostile powers. Winter was anxious to establish his rather overbearing friendliness and Gibbon was equally keen to preserve his neutrality. Neither had the other's welfare much at heart and both were covering up other emotions which inspired them.

"I think you've done quite well, Bert," said Winter after making a full study of all Gibbon's reports; "I can see you've made a good careful job of it. But I think it's made more difficult for you by the fact that you've got to know all these people personally."

"I don't know what you mean by got to know," said Gibbon; "I was born knowing Brendan Hamp pretty well. We went to school together."

"In Balham, eh?"

Gibbon nodded.

"Don't think I came across him myself," frowned Winter. "Not there, anyway. It was my first district so that makes it some time ago. I've got on since then."

"Well, what do you make of it?"

"There's certainly room to do a bit more on the explosion; you've really only skimmed things there, my boy, we'll have a go at that together. Then I can see you're not happy about the Perlott business—well, I know what it is to have a feeling that something's wrong and yet not be able to put your finger on it; all policemen know it, I suppose. We'd better find out more about her. Pity her employer is abroad. Still, there will be ways." He reached out a hand. "Let's see what you've got on her."

The Perlott file was thick and bulky—Miss Perlott had seen to that.

"Hmm," said Winter, "quite a talker, wasn't she? You get 'em like that. Had a woman like this in my district, she died naturally, although I always wondered why. Hmm. Perlott was a local I see, born here; I didn't expect that somehow. Now I wonder why? Why should I have any preconceived idea about her?" He rubbed his chin. "Something there if I can remember." He studied her photograph. "Funny, I remember the name but not the face. Well, it'll come back to me, I suppose. We might go into her background a bit more. Might turn something up. And, of course, if we really come up with anything we'll have to get a post-mortem." He looked pleased, but he put the thought of this pleasure in store away from him. "Meanwhile this may all be just fancy. The explosion is the thing; I don't know that you got all about that you could have done, Bert."

Gibbon grunted; this had always been Winter's way—hand out a compliment with one hand and dig you in the ribs with a knife with the other. However, there was no doubt that he was a fine policeman and keen on his job —possibly too keen.

"What was the name of the expert you called in? Well, we will get hold of him again."

Mr. Madge was delighted to be called in again. There were hardly enough explosions for him these days. People were getting softer, although they do say the I.R.A. are starting up again, he would say wistfully to his friends.

"No trouble, Superintendent," he said, rubbing his hands. "Delighted to assist the cause of justice."

"As to that," said Winter, "I don't know. But about this explosion now?"

"Tricky things explosives, people ought to be more careful."

"I hope you're not suggesting this explosion in the Post Office was an accident," said Winter in alarm.

"Oh no, not at all. The reverse, deliberate I am sure. No, what I meant was that the ignorant or perhaps I ought to say the amateur exploder doesn't realise how he gives himself away. There's a signature, my dear Superintendent, to every explosion."

"Ah, that's the stuff, now I hope you're the man to read the signature."

"I can do my best. I wouldn't like to go beyond what I can be precise about. I can say this, however. You might say there are two main groups of explosives, those containing nitro-glycerine and those not. Dynamite and gelignite—those old friends both contain it."

"Not friends of mine," said Winter firmly.

"And then there are those not in the nitric group. Ammonal is such an explosive, or amatol, used extensively in mine work. These are usually fired by means of detonators containing fulminate."

"I see."

"Then there is TNT—the safest of explosives, when pure. It has, of course, to be pure." He nodded to himself. "Our explosive is not, however, either ammonal or TNT, I should say."

"Well, what is it?"

"My guess is one of the newest synthetics, say Nitropenta or Hexogen R.D.X. The latter, I *think*, with perhaps a slight touch of TNT. I can't be quite sure."

Winter looked grave. "Any more information for me?"

"Well, I guess it was set off by a small electric detonator, standard sort, made every day for the army or mines."

"Professional job, eh?"

"In a way, in a way." Mr. Madge looked puzzled. "The container has me foxed. Can't find much trace. Must have been very thin metal. However, I did find this piece, and also this, and both are almost certainly— there are signs you see—from the container." He held out two pieces of battered blackened torn metal, thin and burnt by fire. One piece was bent into a scroll-like shape rather like the lid of a sardine tin when it has been rolled up, and the other had a neat slit across it, just big enough to push a penny through.

Winter picked up the fragments and studied them. "Mean anything to you?"

Madge shook his head doubtfully. "There's something, but I can't put my finger on it yet. You'd better keep them, Superintendent. I'll put them into a box for you."

Back in Gibbon's office Winter was still thinking about the pieces of tin. He read through Gibbon's report again.

"You didn't have much sort of luck in your personal inquiries, I must say," he said aloud.

"I questioned the Post Office people themselves, of course. There was no one else."

Winter strolled to the window. "You didn't use your eyes, Bert, my boy." He pointed. From where they stood they could look down the sloping curve of the market and see the mock Georgian façade of the Post Office. Winter pointed: "Look."

Opposite the Post Office were two stalls. One was bright with flowers and the other rich with candy floss and hot dogs.

"Those stalls there the day of the explosion?"

"Every day every summer."

"Ask them?"

Gibbon shook his head.

"Didn't do your job properly there, boy. I thought I'd trained you better than that. Use your eyes first, I used to say, before you start asking other people to use theirs. Come on."

Outside the Post Office was Mr. Organ's van and a big lorry loaded with bricks. A large fair young workman was loading bricks on to a little hand trolley.

"Bit of construction?" asked Winter with what passed with him for affability.

"No," said the man in an equally friendly voice, "I'm just going to take these into the Post Office to post them."

"No need to be rude. I asked a civil question."

"No you didn't. Or you didn't mean it civil. I know who you are: you're the cop from London."

It was Winter's introduction to the high spirit of the market and Gibbon watched with grim pleasure. Winter wouldn't be able to push the market around.

Ish Murphy hurried from behind the lorry.

"Now, Fred, just take those bricks round to the back,

me dear, and I'll talk to the policeman." He smiled upon Winter, "Fred's a nice boy but he can't bear policemen —it's his history, poor boy."

"Come up against them, has he? Well, it's up to him, he knows how to keep out of their way, he knows how to keep out of the way of the law. He can judge."

"Yes, indeed, poor boy, it's quite in the family, his father was in your way of business."

Winter looked a shade less confident. "Oh, he was? Maybe I've come across him."

"Oh, you might have done—he's a judge."

Winter ground his teeth; he had not, never had had, a sense of humour, and he was quite unable to see whether he was being laughed at or not.

Don't try the old man too far, warned Gibbon with a look.

"Well, Ish Murphy's me name, the inspector here knows me," said Ish, and he got into the lorry and drove off.

"Was he around the day of the explosion?" asked Winter. "I never trust an Irishman."

"Ish was here all right," said the owner of the candy floss stall who had been taking everything in with interest (he at any rate believed in 'Use your own eyes before you use other people's'). Knocking his way angrily through a group of dogs and small boys—"No, they're not free; no, you can't have a lick"—he came over to the two policemen. "'Course I saw Ish the day of the explosion."

"Oh, you did. What was he doing?"

The man thought. "He was carrying a parcel."

"Oh, was he?" said Winter with emphasis. The bomb could well have been concealed in a parcel.

"Well, it's natural enough in a Post Office, isn't it?

But I know he was, it was a big parcel, it was so big I couldn't see his face."

"You couldn't see his face? You saw him, yet you couldn't see his face? You're a fine witness," said the irate Winter.

"I ain't a witness, I never said I'd be a witness," said the man in alarm. "Here, you let me get back to my stall, the little tykes have got at the hot dogs."

"Why don't you ask him if he saw anyone else?" asked Gibbon mildly. "A man like that might see almost anyone."

Meanwhile the owner of the stall was muttering indignantly to himself and casting dark glances at the two policemen. "Ten bobs' worth gone in a flash; you wouldn't think the little perishers could eat so fast. Now go away, mister." He called across to the flower stall, "Maggie, don't you have anything to do with this pair, they're death to the trade."

Maggie, a little mouse of a woman, was however only too willing to tell Winter anything. She had certainly been there all day yesterday and she had certainly seen everyone go in, perhaps she was a little short-sighted though and her memory was not so good.

"But there were crowds of people," she said brightly, "posting postcards and parcels. I saw ever so many faces I knew, just by sight, you know, but even more that I didn't know."

Winter suppressed his irritation. "But you don't remember anything out of the way?"

"There was the milk," said Maggie after a pause for thought. "That was late, and then, of course, there was the flag day collector."

"The flag day collector," repeated Winter. "When

was that?" His hand went to the box in his pocket where rested the fragments of metal that Mr. Madge had given him.

"Oh, I wouldn't know the time," said Maggie; "I really don't know that I could remember the time. I remember I was thirsty," she added thoughtfully.

"Well, perhaps your stomach will help us to fix the time," said Winter rudely. "Now, was it before breakfast or after breakfast, before you had your dinner, or after?"

"Oh, I'm not here before breakfast, Superintendent, but now you mention it I do believe that it must have been after dinner because I had indigestion and that would be why I was thirsty. We had pork, you know, and that never sits well in my stomach and I had taken some milk of magnesia and that always gives you a thirst, you know, and so I noticed the flag seller because of the ship on the flag. That made me thirstier, you see," she finished triumphantly.

"And when do you have your dinner?"

"Oh, twelve o'clock sharp. Aunty's very punctual."

A little old face poked through the canvas at the back.

"Maggie, you're late to your dinner." The face looked suspiciously at Winter and Gibbon. "I heard you were talking to *men*, so I came over."

"Oh, Aunty, these aren't men, these are policemen."

"That's worse, my girl. You never know what they're up to. Don't talk to them, I say." The bright old eyes were taking them all in. "The police never did me any good that I know. Only one time in my life when I wanted them and then where were they? Over the hills and far away, I know."

"What time did you have dinner yesterday, Mother?"

"Twelve o'clock sharp and so we shall today. And I'm not your mother nor anyone else's, praise be it. Come along now, Maggie, or the pickled herring'll be getting cold."

The two men watched Maggie close the stall, put on her hat and get ready to go off.

Maggie came up for a last word. "I did see him, you know, going in with the collecting box. Was it him that did the explosion?"

"It was a him, a man?"

"Oh yes," said Maggie, "I'm in a state, you know, but I did see him. It's been a shock, you know, this explosion, and Betty Perlott going off like that."

"You knew Miss Perlott, did you?"

"We were at school together; she was older, of course," said Maggie with a little simper. "And not really a nice girl I didn't think."

"I'd like to have asked you about her; it's a pity you didn't know her better."

"Oh, I'm sorry too," said Maggie with sincerity, "but why don't you go to the school? There might be someone there. Yes, Aunty, I'm coming." She scuttled off.

"Maggie's going to have indigestion again," said Gibbon.

The girls' school, the main girls' school in the district to which they went next, was a handsome late, very late (*too* late, some said) Georgian-style building, a style much favoured by the architect responsible for most of the public buildings in Bow-on-Sea.

"Not the sort of school I went to," said Winter who was accustomed to bring out bits of depressing reminiscence in this manner. Most of his junior colleagues by now knew of his youth and early struggles which were known amongst them as the Pilgrim's Progress or Eric or Little by Little. To a man however they rejected the accuracy of his memory.

"I suppose it's all right to come just popping in like this," said Gibbon, who was always nervous about schools and school-teachers, his education also having left its mark on him.

Winter ignored this. It was his opinion that the law must be served and as its servant he, John Winter, would and could penetrate anywhere. His conviction of his own rights brought its success and they were soon marching through shining corridors to the headmistress.

On the way they passed a tall fair girl who gave them a sharp glance. She's thinner than she used to be, thought Gibbon. Looks worried.

"Hello, Jeanie," he said, uneasily conscious that she thought him a fool. As soon as he saw her face go pale he was sorry he had spoken. Already he had seen that look of awareness and comprehension on other faces. Oh God, he thought, not you too. But how could Jean be kept out of things?

The headmistress got to her feet when they came in. She regarded them apprehensively. Perhaps no head-mistress could be entirely free from worry about a call from the police. Her face cleared at once when she learnt that they wanted to see her about an old pupil, and one who was in any case dead.

"Well, of course, I don't remember her, it was before my time; I have seen her, I believe, at Old Girls' Meetings, but I never really knew her." And thank Heaven for that, said her expression—Miss Perlott had that sort of effect on her acquaintances. "You must talk to our

Miss Fairplough. She's an old girl herself and knew Miss Perlott better."

Miss Fairplough remembered Miss Perlott. "Oh, I remember Margaret Perlott," she said; "that was her real name. Betty was just a joke. Rabid, she was, poor old dear, mad as a hatter I always thought. I didn't know her much at school; I was on the academic side, you see, and she took up shorthand and typing although she never made much of it. In those days she lived in Cato Street, and I've an idea she still visited there. Why don't you try?" She laughed. "And I don't believe she was getting married." Like everyone in Bow-on-Sea she knew all the details about the case.

The headmistress saw them out herself. She led them through quiet corridors.

"You keep them hard at it," said Winter admiringly, wishing he could treat his assistants in the same way.

The headmistress smiled. "Oh, we pride ourselves on our outside activities. Concerts, picture galleries and other things. For instance, the flag day here recently was largely organised from this school."

"Was it indeed?" said Winter. He was beginning to think that after all he could see a pattern in the curious events which he was being asked to investigate. He pinched his lips and looked at Gibbon, but Gibbon was avoiding his eyes. He was looking down the corridor where a small figure was kneeling beside a bucket and washing an already immaculate floor. Mrs. Beckett gave them her usual ironic, melancholy stare before returning to her work.

"She gets about," said Gibbon. "I meet her all the time."

The two men strolled off in the direction of Cato

Street. Gibbon's feet ached and he would gladly have gone by car, but Winter spared no one and certainly not his subordinate.

"To my mind the person behind all this is a local," said Winter as they walked. "Strictly local too. An inhabitant of Mariners' Market or Seaman's Rise. And —we'll have to check on this with Mr. Madge, Bert—I bet the bomb was carried in a flag day collecting box."

"Be a bit small, wouldn't it?"

"Well, several boxes, then," said Winter irritably. "The explosions are the key. We have to look for someone with experience of explosives. How many in this district with the right sort of army record?"

"There have been two wars," said Gibbon wearily. "Most of them, I suppose."

Even Winter saw it was difficult to get far on those lines.

Cato Street was a short road; it had once contained perhaps half a dozen houses, most of which were now swallowed up in the Florizel Pleasure Ground, but three little cottages were tucked away at the bottom of the road. Or had been.

In the battered garden of the end cottage a man in fireman's uniform was moodily looking over the fence. The cottage itself was a ruin.

"Come to have a look, have you?" he asked. "Ah well, you should have been here last week. That was a sight. Fire and a half. What with that and the Post Office we didn't know where we were. This place burnt too quick for us. We didn't even get the old girl out. She was gone, poor old soul, when we got here."

"What are you doing here now?" asked Winter suspiciously.

"Well, what are you? This and the P.O. at the same time. I didn't like it, see?"

"Neither do I," said Winter slowly. Gibbon said nothing, but his large fair, gentle face looked sad.

"It's the link-up," said Winter, "between Miss Perlott and the explosion; it's all part of the pattern."

"Yes," said Gibbon unhappily, "someone wasn't taking any chances, were they? Well, we know now for certain that we're looking for a murderer."

"Yes, and what's more, I really believe we can pinpoint the group which contains the murderer. We know where to look. The killer must be among the people whose names have already come into the case. I don't believe in any Mr. X."

"We don't yet know *how* Miss Perlott died, or why."

"No, but I'm getting a few ideas. I think it's time we had a talk with some of the big names in this case—the Hamps, Stephen Bent, Gypsy Cresset and your stage Irishman. And we'd better not forget the young man down from London, William Todd. I've had a look at his war record, and it's interesting. Special Service. You can take it from me that he knows all there is to know about blowing things up and killing. And I'm not forgetting the women, Bert, don't think I am."

"No," said Gibbon with extreme depression, "I know you're not."

CHAPTER TWELVE

"IT'S NOT right," said Poll. "It's not right at all."

She had come forward fiercely as soon as she saw Winter and Gibbon by her brother's side.

"What's not right?" asked Gibbon above the noise of the dancing. Winter appeared silently at his elbow like the Wicked Fairy at the Christening.

"That people like you should be set up in judgment on people like us," said Poll, giving Winter an angry look.

"We won't keep you a minute," said Gibbon awkwardly to Brendan and Todd. To his relief they took this better than he had expected.

"I've got to pop off for a moment," said Todd, giving Hilary a long look. "Business, you know."

"Oh, all right," said Hilary. "You lawyers do work hard. Business must come first, of course."

"What a wonderful wife you are going to make," said Todd admiringly. "Are you sure you'll notice whether I'm there or not?"

"Oh, yes, eventually."

By the door Poll was still arguing. "But this is a wedding," she kept saying. Gibbon uttered a long sentence of which only one word came over to Poll.

"Murder," she cried. "Has it come to that now?" And she looked anxiously around the gathering.

"No need to take you far," said Winter affably.

"Your place is by here, isn't it, Bert? Suppose we go there."

So in Gibbon's own room Winter put the two men through a searching interrogation about their movements on the day of the explosion. But the explosion, Cato Street, and Miss Perlott were never directly mentioned. Even Brendan, who had reasons of his own for keeping quiet, grew restive.

"We've got a right to know what's behind all this. What are you getting at?"

"It's not difficult to work out," said Todd. "The explosion."

"And why are we elected?"

"Well, you're still a reservist," said Winter, "and Mr. Todd here learnt some very special tricks about explosions once. I don't suppose you've forgotten all you knew."

"Contrary to the view you seem to have of the army," said Brendan, "it doesn't hand out free samples of the stuff for you to play with. How would I get hold of explosive? And why?"

"I bet Mr. Todd could still tap a supply," said Winter.

"Maybe," said Todd, "but I certainly have no possible reason for doing so. And *when* are we supposed to have had time? We were in London, you may recall."

"You were both in Bow-on-Sea all that morning and early afternoon. Our evidence is that the explosive was planted then."

"But why should we? What reason could we possibly have?"

Winter chose his words carefully. "You may have wondered how it was that a superintendent of Scotland Yard appeared so promptly on the scene of what was only a suspected crime."

"Oh well," said Todd, "you get all over the place."

Winter ignored him. "The reason is that for some time past we have known that a smuggling traffic has been going on. And we had evidence to connect it with Bow-on-Sea and Chancery Lane. You can see now perhaps why I wanted to speak with both of you? I was most interested, Mr. Hamp, to get the report that you had been seen going into the antique shop in Jarvis Street. A useful establishment, isn't it? We value it too, we pick up quite a lot of information from that little shop. You mustn't be surprised if the police keep an eye on it. It's really too valuable to us for us to let it break down. I believe we'd have to run it ourselves if there was any danger of that"—and he laughed cheerfully at his own joke. No one else did though.

"There's smuggling going on all right," said Todd slowly. "I've come to that conclusion myself, but what I'm thinking of couldn't go through the post. Instead of questioning us, if you take my advice you'll have a word with the Cresset family."

"Such of it as survives," said Winter smoothly.

"You've got more on your mind than the explosion and smuggling, haven't you?" asked Brendan, leaning forward. "I heard the word murder. Is Cresta Cresset dead?"

"I believe not, no, I think she is recovering."

"Then you must mean Miss Perlott," said Brendan, drawing in his breath. "What are we supposed to have done, frightened her to death?"

"It might have been a *fight*," said Winter. "There were tears in her eyes."

"Tears," said Brendan bitterly. "The only thing that could have brought tears to that woman's eyes would have been tear-gas. And *that* stuff the police have."

After this comment, Winter couldn't get rid of them quick enough.

"Have you got any tear-gas?" demanded Winter as soon as the door had closed behind them.

"I really don't think we can have," said Gibbon doubtfully. "Not in my department. We leave that to the uniformed branch."

Winter rang through to the sergeant in charge of the main police station. "You got any tear-gas?"

"Ah, that was before my time."

"I don't think tear-gas could kill even the weakest heart," said Gibbon when the sergeant had gone, but Winter was already telephoning.

"Get me that report you have on her body," he snapped. "You ought to have had a proper medical report done. It's so late now."

Gibbon shuffled through his notes, repressing the thought that if it hadn't been for him no one would have thought of murder. More fool me, he thought grimly. He grinned as he thought of his visit to the doctor. He hoped Dr. Beecham was having a good holiday.

On the telephone Winter had his own private medical adviser, a doctor who thanked his stars almost daily that dug away in his pathology laboratory it was almost impossible for him to meet the detective face to face. He dreamed one day of meeting Winter stretched out on one of his tables. "Gentlemen," he would say to his students round him, "I know this subject, I have never seen the face but I recognise the name." Meanwhile there was the telephone and he and Winter had many a happy chat on it.

"I doubt tear-gas could have killed her," he said absently; he had an interesting problem on hand. "But something on those lines might have helped her along a bit, I suppose."

"Well, it looked as though she'd been crying," said Winter obstinately, "and it seems she wasn't the sort to cry from nature."

"Well, there's always onions, isn't there? No, my dear man, a mere joke. Tell me, as well as inflammation of the nostrils and eyes, were there extensive burns?"

"What's that? Anyway, we haven't got a medical report," said Winter glaring at Gibbon.

"You ought to have had. I'm not a magician. However, from what you say I dare say lung oedema was present."

"Would that have killed her?"

"No, Superintendent dear, not necessarily. Or not quickly anyway."

"Well, what could produce these symptoms and kill her quickly?"

"Have you thought of a death-ray, Superintendent? Or a stranger from another planet? Or maybe she did just die naturally after all"

Winter ignored these pleasantries. He was an experienced policeman and all the creaking apparatus of Miss Perlott's death convinced him that she had not died naturally.

"What could have produced these symptoms and have killed her? I tell you we've got evidence of an explosive being used in this case and I wonder if the person who could use explosive couldn't also use some form of gas."

"He'd find it hard to get hold of."

"But what sort of gas could have done it?" went on the persistent Winter.

"Tell me the physical indications again," said the pathologist, at last taking Winter seriously. "Yes, I see. Well, it couldn't have been one of the newer gases, they have *much* nastier symptoms and you wouldn't need to have a weak heart to die from them, far from it." He thought, "Might be one of the chlorine group. Old-fashioned, you know, but nasty in their way."

"And where would a man get chlorine?"

"I thought you told me not to worry about that. Anyway, you can't. It's out of date and you don't make these things for fun. The last lot would have passed out of the manufacturers' hands in the mid-nineteen-thirties—say round about the time of the Abyssinian War."

"Well, supposing it was stored up?"

"It's not the sort of thing you keep by you in a bottom drawer. Anyway, it's not stable. Fresh or nothing. Deteriorates pretty rapidly after a time."

"I see, well it certainly makes it more difficult, but thank you, doctor." Then a vision of the shining school laboratory to which far too many of his suspects seemed to have access to, rose before his eyes. "Could you *make* it, not at home exactly but with simple equipment?"

"Make it?" The pathologist seemed surprised. "It'd be pretty risky, wouldn't it? Look here, this isn't my subject really, I'll have to get you someone else, we do have a chap who specialises more in that line. But, you know, making poison gas isn't just the sort of thing you learn at school."

"Isn't it now?" said Winter dryly and sat down to wait for his new call. It came in about half an hour.

"Hello," said a cheerful Canadian voice. "The Prof. says you want to know how to run up a mixture of chlorine gas in the home. Well, here comes the recipe . . ." He read out a list of ingredients. Was he laughing? Winter asked himself suspiciously. "Got all that? Well, I think I'd better tell you that you'd have considerable difficulty in producing this in your little kitchen without doing yourself in."

"I see."

"As a matter of fact one old girl did do herself in by cleaning her sink with half a pint or so of liquid bleach plus the better part of a tin of abrasive lavatory powder (she having run out of proper sink cleaning-powder and being mad anyway). Says not to do this *very* clearly on the tin but she had to go one better and before she knew where she was she was saying hello to the angels."

"And you could kill yourself, or someone else that way?" asked Winter with a sort of wonder in his voice.

"Well, it wouldn't be one hundred per cent reliable. What you would be producing would be a sort of pseudo-phosgene gas, basically a carbonyl chloride. It wouldn't have quite the kiss of death of the professional article but it wouldn't be no wind of heaven either, and I wouldn't care to come too close to it. Not for too long."

"Was this other case recent?"

"This summer. Caused no end of a fuss. All the old ladies who might have done the same thing came to the inquest. Coachloads of them. The Prof. did the autopsy. Said the inquest was like a first night."

"It must have been while I was in Paris. And these things the old lady used; they are in common use?"

"Oh lord, yes, stacks of them. Whito, Brightcoat,

Lite—those are a few brand names of the bleaching liquids. And then the lav. powders: well, Vigor was what the old girl used instead of her usual Sinko or Hercules sink powder, and rigor was what it gave her."

Winter put down the receiver and was silent. A completely new picture of the crime was taking shape.

"I think we may have been wrong, Bert," he said absently, "to stress the soldier aspect too much. This seems to be now more of a homely crime."

He continued in thought for a few minutes, remembering some of the things he had learned from the suspects in all their conversations. He now remembered one fact which had hardly seemed important at the time. "Whoever thought this way of killing would want to experiment," he said at last. "And there has been one other puzzling death here. What about the cat?" He got up. "We may have difficulty in getting an exhumation order for Miss Perlott, but damn it, nothing's going to stop me digging up a cat."

Under the watchful ring of eyes poor Hake was disinterred. The Hamp family had been prevented from attending after having given an angry assent to the doctor.

"Do you really expect to get much from this?" asked Gibbon.

Winter shrugged his shoulders. "Nothing maybe. I'm taking a chance."

The report on Hake was rushed through; it was brief and clear. Hake had died from two savage blows on the head, but *before* this he had been subjected to some form of burning stifling gas, his eyes and nose and throat were raw and inflamed—and he had torn his ears in an attempt to relieve the irritation.

Winter put down the report before Gibbon with a satisfied air. "So I was right."

He knew however that the worst part of the task was still ahead of him; he had to find the raw materials that had been used so malevolently, and then he had to construct a proof that would convince a jury.

He was concerned with proof but Gibbon was uneasily occupied with guilt. He had the conviction that this case would not wait upon proof but would burn itself out in another killing.

"I don't see how I can go round all the households and kitchens I'd like to," said Winter, "to see what hell's brews they could mix up in them. Not without a search-warrant and it'd be a bit difficult to ask for that."

"I should have a word with Mrs. Beckett. As far as I can see she works in them all. And she won't have missed anything, not if I know her." Whether she will tell you is another matter, thought Gibbon, but he didn't say so.

"Yes, yes, I'd certainly like to see that old woman. For several reasons it might be a good idea to have a word with her."

Mrs. Beckett lived in a small house not far from Cato Street, not far from the market; strategically placed, as those who believed her to be the *éminence grise* of Mariner's Market said, to keep an eye on everything.

She was sitting in her kitchen enjoying a cup of tea when they arrived.

"Have a cup?" she said companionably, and poured them out cups of thick sweet nourishing tea like soup. "I know what *you've* come about."

"You do?"

"Old Betty Perlott. I knew it was funny her going like that."

"She had a weak heart."

"She'd planned on keeping it going a bit longer. No, someone helped her, I reckon. Mind you, she'd been putting a strain on her heart the way she was going round all excited. You should have heard her after the phone call."

"What call was that?"

"Oh, I know, you think you're getting information out of me, don't you? But supposing I wanted to tell you? I been looking forward to a talk about it. You've been slow. Well, she had this call and she was as pleased as Punch afterwards. They'll get what's coming to them, she kept saying. Well, I reckon she got it herself."

"Could you hear what was being said?"

"Well, only her side, she didn't say much, just a yes and no, but I could see her face."

"Pity you didn't hear his voice," said Winter reflectively. "You might have recognised it."

"Him," said Mrs. Beckett. "Wasn't a him. It was a woman." She paused, and added carefully, "Anyway, it was a female voice."

Gibbon could tell that Winter, however carefully he tried to mask it, was disconcerted, perhaps even shocked. Not so himself. It was what he had been beginning to expect.

"The feminine touch," said Winter ironically. "Well, perhaps it bears out what I had in my mind." He looked round the kitchen seeking for a formula to start the inquiry he had come here to make. As he did so he saw that the shelves were neatly stacked with tins of all household cleaning material. He was looking at Mrs. Beckett's perks from the places she cleaned. She saw him looking.

"Well, people throw things away before they're properly finished," she said defensively. "Not that you can blame them, some of the stuff is such rubbish. Still, waste is waste all the world over. I found this tin of Sinko in the bin, someone threw it away after the funeral; well, that was *wrong*, wicked waste. Say what you like about Miss Perlott, she wouldn't have allowed waste like that. Mind you, it isn't up to much, don't work like it ought, you can't get a rub out of it."

Winter went over and examined the tin. He was careful how he handled it although all prints must have perished long ago.

"Mrs. Beckett," he said solemnly, "you'll never know how close to death you've been."

"Mind you, I exaggerated a bit," he said to Gibbon. "She wouldn't have done herself any damage unless she'd doused the sink with a bleach too. You realised what happened of course? Someone substituted some Vigor powder (or a similar brand) for the original Sinko, which when mixed with the Bleacho, which was the Perlott's well-known and dotty habit to use when cleaning the sink, produced a lethal compound. Then all the murderer had to do was to see there was a mess in the sink and sit back and wait for the old girl to see to her own murder. And there she was victim of her own love of cleanliness."

"And of her own nasty habits," said Gibbon with feeling.

"Don't get too worked up." Winter was really pleased with himself. "I dare say we shall get some prints on this tin. Pity Mrs. Beckett couldn't make an identification."

To Gibbon it was pretty clear that Mrs. Beckett could have made a pretty guess and wasn't doing it.

"Miss Maggie the florist thought it was a man going into the Post Office," reminded Gibbon.

"We'll have a word with her."

But Maggie, faced once again with questioning and without Aunty at her elbow, was not coherent.

"Oh well, I only saw the back, you know," she said. "I wish you wouldn't keep bothering me."

"This is murder," said Winter severely. Maggie gave a shriek. "It was a man now you say. How do you know?"

"Oh well, he was wearing trousers, you know."

Winter groaned. "You live here by the seaside, you're here every summer. Haven't you ever seen a woman in slacks? Was it a man or a woman?"

Maggie burst into tears.

In his mind Gibbon could see Brendan's worried face.

"I don't like to do this to you, Brendan," said Gibbon to himself. "But I think I could put a name to the killer."

CHAPTER THIRTEEN

AFTER THE wedding reception, dragged back to reality, the Hamps had watched the exhumation of Hake with foreboding. Every one of them tried to fit it into the picture of events they were forming, but somehow the champagne and Hilary in a white dress and the smell of flowers would get in the way. It was so difficult, as Poll complained, to know if they were at a wedding or a funeral. Hilary was heedlessly happy and a kind of desperate gaiety had descended upon the others.

The death of Hake meant different things to each one of them. Ruth was thoughtful, Jean was very angry, and Poll seemed to think Hake had somehow done it on purpose to annoy *her*. To Brendan it meant one more sinister fact aimed at him; all the time he had the feeling that he was meant to be the chief sufferer.

"Murder," said Poll with a shiver. "I can't get over that." She looked round at the assembled faces; they were all there, even Hilary and her new husband. "What is it that makes some people kill?"

Brendan shrugged. "There was an adequate motive, I dare say, but how can we tell? Some people are the murdering kind—it's their way out."

"It's worse than the war, isn't it?" asked Poll. "I feel so *nervous*." Then she made an attempt at flippancy, "What did *you* do in the great war, Ruthy darling?"

"Oh, I was in the A.T.S.," said Ruth.

"Can't you just see her," said Poll. "She was one of the *bouncy* ones, and her uniform was always just a little bit too tight."

"You are a cat, Poll," said Brendan.

"I don't mind," said Ruth. "True, I dare say. I was only a kid. I had a lovely time though. I was quite sorry when it was all over. There was always company. Do you know once I had three sergeants all wanting to take me to the same dance on the same night. They had to fight it out, I'm afraid. You choose, boys, I said to them. It was quite exciting. Then the one that won said he had to drink twelve pints of beer to celebrate (I dare say he'd had just a drop before, too)."

"What happened then?"

"Well, he was ever so sick, poor boy, but I didn't hold that against him."

"Still, you must have wished he hadn't kept out the other two."

"Oh, I still had them," said Ruth, surprised. "I went out with them the next night. Or was it the same night? I forget."

"That's the life Ruth likes," said Poll.

"Well, it was a change. I'd been living at home with Mother for seventeen years and that was dreary, I can tell you."

"What did she make of the way her little girl was growing up?"

"I don't know," said Ruth indifferently, "I never went back home again."

"Well, Brendan and I were brought up by loving parents and always told them everything," said Poll, adding gloomily, "But I don't know that our happy home life did much for our characters. Look at us now."

"Speak for yourself," said her brother.

Jean was standing rigidly by the sink. They were all in the kitchen—it was one of the few rooms that did not overlook Hake's now empty grave, and it was early in the morning after Hilary's wedding. But Jean's thoughts were far away. She was remembering the scene last night when she had crept over to tell Stephen about Hake. As it turned out in the end she never had told him.

She had banged on the door of Grey Place and eventually found Stephen in his little study bedroom on the ground floor. Stephen was wearing a stiff dark blue robe of splendid satin.

"Suits me, doesn't it?" he asked with a slight air of preening himself.

"Yes it does, lovely silk."

"My father had it made for him in China. Now I'm wearing it"—he winked—"in secret, of course. The old man'd have a blue fit if he knew. There's a nasty mean streak in him and he's looking for a chance to take it out of me. He never has liked me, not that I blame him for that altogether, still I return the compliment. It might have been better if my mother had lived, but I doubt it. The truth is I don't like him and he doesn't like me." He paused to stroke the rich silk. "You don't think this dressing-gown looks—well, womanish?"

"No." Jean was definite.

"Because I wouldn't like that. Isn't it lovely the way the silk slides over the skin? Feel it. Go on, stroke it like that, delicious, isn't it?"

"Yes," agreed Jean, withdrawing her hand. "Oh, Stephen, you've torn up one of your pictures."

"Broken. It was in oil on wood. I shall burn it."

"Oh, but why?"

He shrugged. "Why do you think? It was rubbish. The painting was dark and muddy and the design, oh, that was a failure. I felt inspired when I started it. This is going to be *good*, I thought, the best ever, and then after the first few minutes I knew it was as bad as the rest." He sat down on the bed, "I know I'm not a painter, I don't deceive myself, but if only I was bad in a good sort of way. If only I could say to myself—'Boy, you can't paint but you've got life and imagination into it all the same.' But that's just what there wasn't—it was as dead as mutton." He kicked the painting.

Jean bent down. "Well anyway, let me see."

Stephen knocked her hands away. "No, don't. I'd rather you didn't. It was rather a special painting."

Jean rubbed her wrist.

"Did I hurt you? Here, let me look"—and he pulled her down beside him. "Oh, nothing there at all."

"Funny little fish," he said and kissed her.

"I'd better go now."

"Yes, you'd better go." Stephen stood up and gave her a little pat. "But I'll be across to see you in the morning, right early. So get up and wait for me." He grinned. "Wild horses couldn't keep me."

But the morning had ticked on and there had been no sign of him, and Jean's temper, never very certain, had got sharper and sharper.

Poll's voice broke into her thoughts. "What are you standing like that for?" She, too, was irritable this morning.

"She's waiting for Godot," said Brendan leaning forward to light a cigarette.

"I'm waiting for Stephen," said Jean fiercely, "and there's no need for any of your funny remarks."

176

"My remark was not funny," said Brendan. "More's the pity."

"Yes, Stephen is late," said Poll. "But there, he's an artist, that boy, nothing could make him punctual."

"Oh, he's not so bad," said Ruth tolerantly.

Jean looked grim.

"If you continue to look like that he'll wonder why he wasn't later."

Ruth got up. "I'm off to have my hair washed. See you all later. Brendan, if I'm later than twelve you might come and pick me up. I have some errands to do so I might be."

"And we can do the clearing up," said Poll.

"What about Mrs. Beckett?" asked Brendan.

"You don't suppose she'll be fit for much after the day she had yesterday?"

An hour later the house was a good deal cleaner, but Jean was still standing angrily looking out of the window.

"Don't look like that," advised her aunt.

"I hate him." And she looked it.

"He'll be here soon," said Poll. And sure enough there was Stephen coming in the gate now. "Here he is."

"And I won't go out now Certainly not," said Jean sitting down.

Poll met Stephen at the door. "You don't look as though you'd got over the party yet," she said accusingly. "And your girl friend's in a tearing temper."

"Yes, I am a bit late but it couldn't be helped."

"Well, if I was you I should escape while the going's good."

"What? No, I couldn't do that."

"If you think I'm going to go anywhere with you, you're mistaken," shouted Jean through the door.

177

"There's little sweet and gentle," said Poll wearily. "Take her out before she pulls us to pieces."

"Cooeee," said a gay voice from the door. It was Gypsy wearing a bright green jersey and a lavender skirt. She carolled a little, then did a little dance. "Cresta's better," she said. "Isn't that lovely. Am I in voice today?"

"Yes," said Poll a trifle grimly. If she was going to have Gyp on top of everything, she was not pleased. "Too much so."

"I do hope so," said Gypsy, not taking offence for once, "I've got a summer job." They stared at her.

"I'm singing (anyway they said I *can* do some singing) at the Wee Tots Theatre in Peter Pan's Playground down on the beach."

"Wherever's that?" asked Poll.

"*You* know. It's down by the Pleasure Ground, in fact it's part of the Pleasure Ground. Of course it's not very well paid, but Ish says——"

"Oh, Ish."

"It was Ish helped me to get it—he's got friends everywhere, that boy, he'll go far."

"He'll go too far one day," said Poll.

"Oh, you needn't be nasty about him, he's always stuck up for you. I won't talk about my friends, he says, when Old Organ says one of you done in Miss Perlott."

"That was good of him."

"Of course he did say you'd be well advised not to go out more than you can help, and that's why I popped in to see if you want any shopping done. I do believe in being neighbourly."

Poll looked hard at Jean and Stephen. "Well, children," she said cheerfully, "if you don't go out for your walk soon you'll miss all the nice people. Oh, don't hurry, Gypsy, they're going just your way. Take the old vixen down with you," she whispered fiercely, "and don't let her talk to anyone on the way. I won't be responsible for what will happen if Brendan hears her talking like that. The fool."

With worried faces Jean and Stephen went off with a reluctant Gypsy. Poll, left alone, sank back delighted. "Three birds with one stone," she told herself. "After ten minutes of Jean and Stephen in the mood they were in, old Gypsy won't go tattling round any more. Jean looked at her as if she could eat her up."

The gloss wore off Poll's self-satisfaction a little.

The market was full to overcrowding with holiday-makers. Jean had Gypsy tight by the arm and was talking to her in a friendly fashion—the friendliness of the octopus which can't bear to let go and "this hurts me more than it hurts you".

"Don't pull so," said Jean mildly. "You make me frightened I'm hurting you."

"Oh no, dear," gasped Gypsy, tears almost in her eyes. "No, not a bit, I've always been a good friend to you, dear, haven't I? I used to say what a good girl you were when hardly anyone else did."

"Thanks, Gypsy," said Jean laconically, "I always like to know what my friends think of me."

"Oh, you're so clever, dear."

Gypsy's eyes were darting round looking for help or Ish, not that Ish would be a help of course, but a new tormentor would be a change.

"Of course I know you're clever," she said. "But be careful, dear, you know what I always say—if you can't be good be careful." And she gave a little bass titter.

179

"You're a big girl now, Gypsy, to play such nasty games," said Jean, releasing her arm suddenly, "and to have such nasty thoughts. A nasty big girl."

"Oh, I didn't mean anything. You're putting words in my mouth," said Gypsy. "'Bye, Stephen, 'bye, Jean, see you later"—and she darted off glad to be free. She wasn't free for long however because Ish was waiting for her a few feet away.

"She is an old vixen," said Jean. "Poll had the right word. She thinks one of us killed Miss Perlott, damn her."

"I believe you egged her on for some reason though," said Stephen. "It certainly looked that way to me."

"I wanted to see how far she'd go. Better to say it to us than go sneaking round to other people." She paused. "Wonder what she meant though; she meant something."

"Oh, I don't know, she was just being mysterious, I think."

"Gossip certainly follows the Hamps round," said Jean ruefully. "Poor old Dad thinks it all comes from something he did in the past, years ago. He never talks about it but Hilary and I know what it means when he gets gloomy and tells us it's a pity we were ever born. Dad's Oedipus complex, we call it."

"That's something different," said Stephen.

"Oh, I know, don't act so educated."

"That's fine coming from you."

They were now bickering quite happily just in the way they used. Jean smiled cheerfully. Gypsy had fulfilled her purpose and so, it occurred to her, had Poll.

"Poll's no ball of fire intellectually," she said thoughtfully. "But she knows how to manage people." At that moment she looked remarkably like her father.

The Florizel Pleasure Ground lay open before them.

No money to pay for admittance but nothing was free once you were inside. If you take a deep breath in there they charge you for it, Poll had once declared angrily. Roughly a triangle, it was bounded on one side by Mariners' Market and on the other by Cato Street and stretched out to the sea on the third side. It was crowded with holiday-makers and the buzz was going round about the murder. One little area of the Pleasure Ground was devoted to food and drink and Stephen pulled Jean in this direction.

"Let's go and have a fizzy drink." He beckoned towards where the owner of the lemonade stall stood pouring his poison out to his patrons. He also provided great bowls of well-salted potato crisps and bits of nuts "All free," as he would say generously, but actually they were to take the taste away.

"I didn't think you drank such stuff."

"Well, it's habit-forming. There's a lot you don't know about me anyway. I've learnt to like the dear stuff. It was silly not drinking. Childish."

"Stephen, you sound just like Aunt Poll."

"Do I? Not a bad way to sound."

"No," agreed Jean doubtfully. "No, I suppose not."

The prosperous proprietor leaned forward and served them personally. "'Morning, sir, and how are you? Nice to see the young lady. New friend, eh? How would you like it, cool, cold or down-right frosted?"

"Don't bother to think, Jean," said Stephen. "It's all the same anyway—tepid."

"I've got a nice little fridge down here, sir," said the man reproachfully.

"I know, but you're too economical to use it."

"Takes a farthing off my profits every ten bottles,"

said the man. "Well, I ask you. We got to fight in-
flation. And people is very suggestible. Cold, I says,
and they says cold and they think it *is* cold."

"More fool them."

"Anyway, it isn't good to eat things too cold," said
the economist with an air of virtue. "Sends the
digestive tract into a spasm."

Jean and Stephen did not go unobserved. Superintendent Winter and Inspector Gibbon were also in the
Pleasure Ground. This was a stroll that Gibbon frequently took as a matter of routine. It was his experience
that what the Pleasure Ground knew today he knew
tomorrow. Gibbon was proud of his district although
he spurned the use of the metropolitan term "manor" and
mentally dubbed it his "bailiwick". He was proud of
its enterprise and spirit. His pride in it had been chiefly
responsible for keeping him free from corruption.
Winter had been quite right—the inspector had certainly
been offered pickings. He had never taken them, and
so far as he knew none of his men had either, and his
conscience was so far clear. But Gibbon knew that he
had fallen into other practices and he shifted uneasily
away from Superintendent Winter. He had no hope
beyond the hope that it would not all come to light—he
simply hoped he would behave himself with dignity when
it did. He thought of Poll with affection and misery.

The paths of the two couples came nearer and nearer
to the Peter Pan's Playground. It was full of delights
for the little people.

"Nothing like this in my day," said Winter sourly.
"Bit of an old box on wheels and thought ourselves
lucky." The reminiscences of Superintendent Winter
varied with his mood but Gibbon felt fairly sure that

Winter, a neat prim little boy, had never been allowed near an old box on wheels.

They were approaching the paddling pool, which was full of shouting children, throwing water over each other and over a much harassed attendant. Beyond the pool was a miniature railway, run apparently by the Seven Dwarfs although a closer look under the little caps and beards might have revealed angry adult faces.

Beyond the railway was a white wall and from this direction came the sound of voices, raised in a sort of singing.

This was the Tiny Tots Theatre, where for the small sum of sixpence any child could have an audition over a microphone and then, if good enough, entertain its fellows from the stage (only no known child had within living memory ever been known to fail). As none of the audience ever listened—being much too preoccupied with their own performance past or to come—it really did not matter what sort of noise was made. Only the people in the neighbouring houses complained occasionally, saying it worried the dog or woke the baby or even once that the milk was curdled.

Jean and Stephen leaned over the low white wall to look and listen.

"I suppose this is where Gypsy has her summer job," said Jean, looking round, "but I can't see her anywhere, can you?"

There was a little knot of people standing near the entrance, guarding the sixpenny way in from the on-slaughts of the penniless but hopeful. Among them was a sturdy figure dressed in white silk with blue spots, but Jean might be forgiven for not recognising Gypsy, for the face was obscured by a large frilly sun-bonnet.

There was a small riot going on round the entrance.

Eventually a large hefty man emerged from the crowd which melted through the gate, and came to rest against the wall by Stephen and Jean. He was breathing heavily and there was a long scratch across his nose. After a rest he took out a cigarette and began to smoke.

"Kids," he said with deep feeling as he caught Stephen's eyes. "They'll kill me yet."

"But why take this job on if you hate children?"

The manager took three long draws at his cigarette in order to give himself strength for speech.

"Oh, I did like 'em all right once before I started here. I wasn't mad keen, didn't ever want them to come too close, but I thought they was *human*. Even at the beginning I used to say to meself, Ted, these kids you get here may not look much but they'll grow up a normal human being same as you or I." He sniffed and patted at his wall eye. "Well, I was wrong. The way all the kids here carry on is animal. We certainly see life in the rough here all right."

From over the wall came the sound of the stamping of many angry little feet.

"I'd better get back and start it," he said, popping his cigarette into his mouth again, "or they'll eat me."

As he went off he was observed to be limping.

"Here I am, kiddies," they heard him shout over the microphone. "Here's Uncle, now step up, dears, and let us hear your voices over the mike. Go on, give us a hand," he shouted to the figure in blue and white standing at the back of the platform.

"Look, that's Gypsy," said Jean.

"Are you sure?"

"Maybe I can't see her face. But I'd know that figure anywhere."

184

Gypsy rounded up the children into some sort of order. As far as could be seen she put the largest and toughest at the top of the queue and the smallest and weakest at the end, but it was not clear how far she was a free agent and it may simply have been the course of natural selection.

Once organised she kept well clear of the line and presently it could be seen that she too was limping. She was also muttering to herself.

The first small singer swaggered out on the platform and grabbed the microphone.

"Here I am, Mum," he shouted. "Here I am, aren't I smashing?"

He then began to sing.

"Tone deaf," said Stephen.

The occupant of the stage sang straight through the chorus of "Davy Crockett" three times and was beginning it again when the manager and Gypsy limped on to the stage and carried him off—still singing—between them.

He was followed by a little girl who seemed to have no relations in the audience, for no screams of encouragement greeted her nor did she wave to anyone, but with a grim look she put her face right up to the microphone and sang the first words of "Lily Marlene". At intervals she released the microphone and, still singing (only mercifully no one could hear), danced a few steps of tap dancing. At no point did she pause for breath and her colour was beginning to rise.

"She's tone deaf too," said Stephen.

The child was now singing with desperate determination, she hung grimly on to one note, her face went purple and she collapsed, winded, across the stage.

But before her limp form could be removed by the

185

manager and Gypsy, her successor had rushed from the wings, grabbed the microphone from her exhausted but still tenacious grasp and raised up his voice in song.

"*He*'s tone deaf," said Stephen. "They're all tone deaf."

The girl, who was being nervously removed by Gypsy, sat up and protested that she hadn't had her full turn. She delivered Gypsy a disabling kick and put her hands on the microphone. Still singing, the little boy who was now doing his turn gave his rival a sharp blow. The manager rushed on to the stage and after him rushed the rest of the queue of children.

The audience, which was largely made up of parents, stood, hesitated, then rushed for the stage too.

"I say," said Stephen, "do you think this happens every day?"

It looked as though it did for the manager had developed a simple technique for dealing with this problem. He simply threw everyone off the stage as quickly and methodically as possible, kicking back those who showed signs of wanting to climb on again. He was no respecter of persons and at one point Jean and Stephen saw Gypsy anxiously trying to crawl back on to the stage.

"Now our singing mistress of ceremonies will give us a song while we get our breaths back," he bellowed cheerily, giving a quick cuff to a little boy who was sneaking round the back. Then he looked round, "Come on, Gyp, where the hell are you?"

"Here," said an exhausted whisper from the ground where Gypsy was patiently trying to climb back on to the stage.

"Well, come on, what do you think you are supposed to be doing, resting?"

Gypsy staggered on to the stage, grabbed the microphone with a sickly smile and began to sing. Owing perhaps to nerves and fatigue, her voice was lower than ever.

The manager endured it for a few bars before bursting out, exasperated: "Here, we can't have a Mother Fairy with a voice like King Kong. Get it up, miss, get it up."

In despair Gypsy produced a banshee wail.

Several of the younger children howled with fear and one child bit his mother. Another came up and bit Gypsy.

The manager stopped playing the piano. "It's no good, miss," he said, "it's no good. You'll have to go. I'd keep you on here if I could but I'd have the kiddies raving."

The platform was crowded again and one child stood heavily on his foot and remained standing on it. Smiling, the manager addressed the boy's mother, "Your poor little fellow is standing on my foot. Get off, sonny." The woman muttered something. "Wot, not your boy? Get off my foot, you little perisher."

The boy leapt away, grabbed at the microphone, missed it and fell against Gypsy. She went heavily to the floor and the microphone fell on top of her.

"Lor', has it hurt you?" asked the manager as he got her up.

"Well, it ain't done me any real good," sobbed Gypsy, almost weeping. "I'm going home."

Alone among the spectators Superintendent Winter noticed that the boom on which the microphone hung was swinging perilously over Gypsy and might soon hit her. He rushed down the centre aisle, moving rapidly for him.

"Miss," he said in a large clear voice. "Miss, I must warn you . . ."

"Oh God!" screamed the much-tried Gypsy. "The police. I don't want to go to prison, I'll turn Queen's evidence, Superintendent. It wasn't my fault."

"Can't you keep your mouth shut, Gypsy?" said Ish emerging from the back of the stage.

"Well, I wasn't planning to arrest you two just yet," said Winter almost gleefully. "But since you ask me to question you, I must."

When they got to the police station Winter—Gibbon felt bitterly, he had almost taken over the running of the place—put Ish and Gypsy into separate rooms.

Gypsy was placed in a small office, turning out a reluctant constable who was doing his nails with a steel file. Ish was urged into an even smaller room which smelt strongly of its last occupant, a female spaniel.

"Ah, I see you've got rid of the dog, constable," said Winter jovially, to the nail-parer.

"Yes, sir," said the man doubtfully. The dog was in fact in a cupboard. "Bitch it was, sir."

"I'm allergic to dogs," said Ish.

"The dog's gone."

"You can't do this to me, I'm a citizen of Eire."

"I doubt if you are an Irish national. But if you are then you can telephone for the consul." Ish was silent at once.

The superintendent departed to make three telephone calls—two were trunk calls to London and the third and last was a local call.

Hilary and Todd were setting out on their honeymoon again. Their departure was being speeded in true Hamp style. As a result they were already very late.

"You've forgotten your fur coat," said Poll.

"Oh, I'm not taking it."

"I put it in," said Todd, "thinking you'd want it."

"I'll move it out," said Poll helpfully. "Oh, that's right, Brendan, *you* move it. There it is in the back— oh dear, that's Buster! There," she said much gratified. "He knew you were his master, he's hardly bitten you at all. He is a clever dog."

"He did his best," said Brendan mildly, "but I wasn't really co-operating. I don't complain, but I shan't inter- fere with him again."

"I'm not taking Buster on my honeymoon," said Todd firmly.

"Well, dear," said Poll, "I don't know how we are going to get him out. It's that fur coat. I ought to have remembered that he had a passion for it. It reminds him of something!"

"Perhaps it was his mother," said Brendan. "If it's the coat I remember, it easily could have been. They look alike."

Todd advanced, put two arms around Buster, heaved, and with an angry roar Buster was out. He tried to nip Todd who skilfully evaded him by stepping behind his bride.

"Oh, Todd," said Hilary dolefully, a tear beginning to form in her eye, "I don't know if I want to go." The ready tears began to flow and very soon Poll was sniffing too.

The telephone rang and Mrs. Beckett appeared at the door waving to Todd. He went into the house and re- appeared in a few moments.

"Calm yourself, Hill, you can dry up. We're not going. Winter wants me down at the police station."

Todd set off in his car. He was sorry to be leaving

189

Hilary but, by God, he was glad to be getting a crack at Gypsy and Ish at last. Absently he wiped the back of his neck which seemed to be wet. Behind him Buster put in a satisfied tongue.

At the police station he was ushered into Inspector Gibbon's office and left there alone. He sat there for ten minutes, twenty, then thirty, the hour ticked away. Todd smoked incessantly and thought hard; occasionally he consulted his notes.

In her little room Gypsy had wept off all her plentiful make-up and was still crying. In his room Ish was sneezing and mopping his running eyes—he had not invented his allergy to dogs. At intervals there was a whine and a scratch from the cupboard where the other occupant of the room was imprisoned.

At the end of an hour the superintendent, much refreshed by a cup of tea, returned to the room where Todd sat waiting for him. In a few minutes Gypsy and Ish were shown in too.

"Now, Mr. Todd," said Winter, rubbing his hands, "a few days ago you made a few suggestions to me about Miss Cresset and Mr. Murphy. Would you mind repeating them now?"

Todd hesitated.

"Look at him," said Ish, "he can't."

"Ask them what they did with all the girls that Cresta Cresset used to take out on her singing tours? Ask them where they went and what the price was?" He produced his file of papers. "Now listen to this quotation sent me by my sister from the *Melbourne Mail:* 'Ten girls came out to Australia but only two go back. "My wandering girls," said Miss Cresset. "Why do I never get my dancers back home again?"'" Well, why don't she, Ish? Where do the girls go? I'm not saying that they stay in South Africa or Australia or wherever dear Cresta sets foot, but how much farther east do they go? What does it add up to? Let me tell you."

"Do," said Ish.

"What the papers call white slaving."

"What, me?" said Ish indignantly. "Me that's a Trade Unionist, and member of the Leage of Pity and a Brother of the Little Order of Mary? Why, I couldn't do it! And Gyp, look at her and ask yourself."

"Oh, we wouldn't ever have done anything as wicked as that," sobbed Gypsy. "Fancy you thinking we could. We never harmed a soul."

"Except perhaps a few diamond merchants," said Winter cynically.

"Oh, they were all insured. Stands to reason they would be."

"Shut up, Gypsy," said Ish.

"Don't you, miss," said Winter encouragingly. "It'll come easier for you if you talk. I know all about it anyway."

"What is all this?" asked an angry Todd.

Winter hardly glanced at him. "Oh, I don't deny they've been up to something, Mr. Todd, but not what you thought. It's jewels they've been smuggling, not women. Now you study those newspapers you had from all your friends and relations again. What do you find, reading them with a new eye? Pearls from Japan via Australia, diamonds from South Africa and rubies from Central Africa—all, or most of them carried in by Cresta, *on* Cresta, mixed up with the load of false costume jewellery she always wore. Who is going to notice the one real diamond in a glitter of paste? All her false jewellery was cleverly made up for her by that industrious Mr. Pearly Nikoliades who was the brains of the whole large organisation. Even Cresta's part in the whole is a small one, and these two here, and the old man Pickering in London are very small fry." Winter gave them a scornful look.

"Here," said Ish indignantly, "we had a lot of responsibility."

"Well, I'm glad you've explained," said Todd with some bitterness. "If I'd known what a nice clean game they were in I don't know if I wouldn't have joined in myself rather than take a high moral line."

"Oh, you are well out of it. It's a tricky game. Miss Cresta was in a fine state of nerves and so was old Pickering. It was he, by the way, who frightened her with the story that the police were waiting for her at Victoria the day you were to meet her there."

"Old Pickering," said Todd grimly. "Yes, I knew he was in it up to his neck. I was so frightened that he would somehow harm Hilary. I thought she was just the girl to rush where angels fear to tread. I thought she knew more than she did, you see. I was so keen to marry her quickly to keep her safe."

Everyone in the room heard the sound of a powerful car drawing up. Gypsy and Ish looked hopeful.

A large black Rolls was drawing up outside the police station. Out got a little man in a dark suit. It was old Pickering.

"Damn it," said Todd, "the old man's a millionaire."

"No, that's not his car," said Winter with a smile. "It belongs to his organisation. It's a staff car. He's put a bit away, a nice little sum no doubt, but he isn't buying any Rolls. No, old Pickering's what they call a runner or messenger, but he isn't one of the high-ups."

A second car drew up, and Winter looked satisfied. "Ah, that's Jimmy Drew, the chief inspector investigating Frauds and Revenue swindles. I telephoned for him and old Pickering to come at once. Now we shall get on like a house on fire." He beamed at Ish.

"Thanks," said Ish, "but you can't expect me to forget that it's my house you're burning."

"Will they go to prison?" asked Todd of Gibbon as he was shown out.

"Don't you believe it," said Gibbon sourly. "That old man that's come down from London in the car'll get 'em off somehow."

"Will he?"

"Hasn't been hanging around you lawyers all these years without picking up a few dodges."

"No, I suppose not."

"Anyway, it's not our case now. We hand it over to Frauds and Smuggling now. But you'll see Ish and Gypsy back with you, don't worry." His voice was bitter. "It's me you ought to be worrying about."

"Eh?"

"Forget it."

Gibbon waved good-bye and went back to the office for what he knew was coming.

The room was empty, Gypsy and Ish having departed presumably for a talk with Chief Inspector Drew. The door opened and Winter came back in.

"How long have you known what Ish Murphy was up to?" said Winter quietly.

Gibbon swallowed, "For some weeks now," he said. "I wasn't sure though."

"Then you weren't trying," said Winter. "You could easily have been sure. You can't play friends in the police."

"It didn't seem my business," said Gibbon looking out of the window. "I'm a policeman, not a universal conscience."

"Well, make better friends," said Winter without malice.

Gibbon recognised the tone and drew a deep breath; he was reprieved—more, he was declared not guilty. He drew out a handkerchief and mopped his brow.

"D'ye find it hot in here?" asked the superintendent with a surprised air, and this was the only punishment he meted out.

"All this business hasn't got us any nearer the murder of Miss Perlott," he went on, "except that we can be pretty sure it wasn't Ish Murphy and Gypsy Cresset. Gives them a superb motive all right, but Gypsy Cresset would have poured it all out under or even without questioning, and she stuck to it they were together discussing what she calls business when the bottles were planted in the kitchen at Grey Place."

"Even Gypsy wants to save her own neck," observed Gibbon.

"She was telling the truth," said Winter. "Ted Organ bears her out. They met in his jazz club to talk things over. Funny about that accident he met with. I don't suppose we shall ever get to the bottom of that."

He was thoughtful, something to do with Ish but how he was not certain.

"That old soul in Cato Street could have told us a thing or two, I expect," he said thoughtfully. He got out the notes of the interviews he had had with the fire-man and constable concerned. He drummed on the table in front of him. "My God," he said, "I've been a fool. Never do a job slovenly, Bert. I should have asked for a medical report on the body, then I should have been all right. As it was I took too much for granted."

Gibbon was puzzled. "Do you think she was killed in the same way as Miss Perlott then?"

"That's just what I don't think," said Winter. "Think again." He got up. "This is where we start to make up for lost time."

"Cato Street?"

Winter nodded. "But the telephone first."

"Hello!" said the voice over the telephone. "No: Three Area Fire Station speaking."

Winter identified himself.

"What did you say, sir? Oh sorry, sir, that was my men sliding down the greasy pole; speak up, sir, I can't hear you."

"Were you the officer in charge at the time of the fire in Cato Street?" shouted Winter.

"Well, yes I was, you're lucky to get me; I'm going on holiday tomorrow."

"I notice that you said when I questioned you 'But we were too late, the poor old soul was gone when we got there'."

"That's right."

"Now how did you know? Did you see the dead body yourself?"

"Dead? I didn't say she was dead, I said she was gone." The voice stopped and made an indistinguish-able noise to someone. "Sorry, sir, another little inci-dent. I shall have to be off. But she wasn't dead, you know, just gone."

"I ought to be ashamed of myself," said Winter. "Not dead, just gone. Now it's up to us to find her."

Cato Street was stretched before them in the hot sun. They approached the only cottage still inhabited.

"Neighbours always know," said Winter. A uniformed constable strolled up, saluted, and said in a low voice, "Nothing to report, sir."

"I don't quite see this," said Gibbon. "I don't see why it's top priority to find out where the old thing went."

"Don't you? Not *where* she went, but *why* she went, that's the question. Even nervous old ladies (and I've met some old dears that weren't nervous but were more like old sharks) don't just disappear because of a fire. She was frightened and I want to know why she was frightened."

In the front garden of the only occupied house two tiny figures were at work. To the two puzzled men they looked from the back as if they were children; they were working however with a most unchildlike precision and skill and the cackle of laughter which floated over presently was far from that of a child.

"Midgets," said Gibbon awestruck, "midgets from the Pleasure Ground."

When a face was turned, however, it was clear that they were not midgets but just very little old people, tiny nut-brown old people, with eyes as sharp and bright as squirrels. They had something of the squirrel's darting eager way with them.

Winter opened his mouth to ask what he wanted of them but the old man got in first.

"You're the police, aren't you? Come to ask about our fire; 'bout time, too."

"Might have been dangerous," cackled the old woman.

"Was dangerous," said the old man stoutly. "Singed our window curtains. Still, we got the insurance." He gave the two men a bright-eyed look. "Funny fire it was. Sudden, poor old Ma Flower."

"Ah yes, it was her I wanted to ask you about. Can you let me have her address?"

"Can't let you have what I haven't got, mister."

"I'm surprised she didn't let you know where she was going."

"Ah well, she was in a hurry I reckon," said the man, with another burst of laughter.

"So it seems. Why?"

"Nasty old fire, mister. I reckon you'd be in a hurry with that behind you." There was still mirth in the old face.

"I want to trace her."

"Well, she were insured like us. I do reckon she'll come round to claiming for all the damage she had done."

"She will for sure," agreed the old woman.

"You wait till she pops up to claim her insurance."

"That'll take time," said Winter, "and I need her in a hurry."

The bright old eyes looked at him. "Flower was the name and flower's the nature," he said with a final burst of laughter before turning away to his gardening. "Here, catch a potato, Gert."

"Now what was the meaning of all that?" asked Winter as they walked away.

"They thought she laid the fire herself for the insurance," said Gibbon, "*and* they know where she is or could give a good guess but they aren't going to give her away. They came pretty close to saying it though, I thought."

"Mmmm," agreed Winter. "They meant something, I agree."

They were passing the Pleasure Ground and Winter looked up and saw the name spelling itself out in flickering coloured lights. "The Florizel," it said, "Bow-on-Sea's Own Pleasure Ground."

The superintendent put two facts together—two names—Mrs. Flower and the Florizels. "There's too many flowers here," he said, "and I rather suspect one of them is anxious to blush unseen."

A red-haired woman was polishing the brass in front of an old-fashioned merry-go-round. She gave them the sort of sharp-eyed unobtrusive look the market gave to people it had never seen before and thought it might be worth while seeing again. What's in it for me? the look seemed to say. Then she gave him a wink.

The inspector closed his eyes in horror. Paris had not prepared him for this.

"What's happened to the Old Dad?" she inquired of Gibbon.

"Got something in his eye."

"Oh!" She looked at him, "Oh well, that's nasty. Here, let me help." And she produced a bright red handkerchief decorated with kissing lips and cupid bows.

Winter opened his eyes smartly and wrenched his head back, "I'm looking for someone," he said.

"Oh," said the woman, "I dare say we all are really. Who do you think you are, Billy Graham?"

It was many years since the superintendent had undertaken this sort of inquiry himself; these days he would simply send along a constable or at most a sergeant, but today he was in a hurry. It was all the more annoying therefore that he was doing so badly.

"I want Mrs. Flower," he said, "I think you know her."

The woman did not deny this.

"Can you tell me where she is?"

"I wouldn't know, haven't seen the old thing around for days."

But in spite of herself her eyes flickered over the crowd, and fixed themselves on a certain spot.

Pushing through the crowd came Maggie, the owner of the flower stall. She was carrying a jug of beer and some jellied eels. She was in a hurry and muttering anxiously to herself.

Another fact fell into place in the superintendent's mind. Florizel—Flowers—Florist.

"Aunty!" he said with conviction, and stepped smartly forward.

CHAPTER FOURTEEN

MRS. FLOWER showed every sign of wanting to scuttle away but her five feet nothing made no headway against the long angry strides of Superintendent Winter.

"Can't you see when a lady don't want to stop?" she asked angrily as she was checked in her rush.

"Just a word, Mrs. Flower," said Winter.

"I haven't done a thing wrong, whatever those old sharp eyes next door to me have told you; I know what they think."

"They didn't say a thing."

"No more they should do. I've been a good neighbour to them for thirty years and we've never had a quarrel, not that I'll say anything about the way they've quarrelled with each other. Lord, the walls fair shook sometimes. He married beneath him and that's a fact although looking at him you might wonder if it was possible. Still, he's a decent sort, provided you don't..."

"About your fire," interrupted the superintendent.

"Weren't my fire particularly," said the old lady sulkily, "I didn't order it."

"No, of course not."

"No more I didn't. I thought that old couple wouldn't let you get away without passing that thought on."

"I didn't believe it, Mrs. Flower."

"I should hope not. My furniture may be insured; well, I've got some valuable little bits that me old husband left me, but who'd be rolling up to collect the money if I was burnt up with them? Me niece, that's who, and why should I hand over to the skinny girl? I wouldn't run the risk. Besides, I don't need the money. I've got a nice little bit of me own."

"I really do believe you, Mrs. Flower, but why are you so certain it wasn't an accident. Might you not have started it yourself by accident?"

"I was having a cup of tea," said Mrs. Flower, "and it come at me like an explosion."

It was an explosion, thought the inspector, remembering the technique used at the Post Office.

"But you were expecting something to happen, weren't you? You were, weren't you?" he repeated.

He put his question again. Maggie cluttered the jug of beer nervously and looked at her aunt.

"I've been ever so nervous," whispered the old thing. "Ever since——"

"The Post Office fire?"

"No, before that, long before that. Ever since something happened to Betty Perlott."

There was a moment's pause.

"She was an old friend of yours?"

"I don't know that you could call her a friend—she didn't have friends much. I believe she had *one* when she was a girl but they didn't stay friends and you could see why. She was so nosy she couldn't see someone spit without going to look, and nasty too."

"She sounds it," said Winter.

"No, she weren't a friend, but she was a cousin, see, a sort of cousin. Blood's thicker than water, they say. Not that hers was, still we kept in touch." She nodded. "Couldn't bear to think there was something about me she didn't know, you see."

"Omnivorous, eh?"

"Well, she had her taste," said the old lady cryptically.

"Gossips and priers of that sort usually have. There's usually *one* thing above all that they're after."

"There isn't as much of that round here as you might think," observed Mrs. Flower. "I don't mention the summer visitors though, what they does, the Lord alone knows."

"So it made it all the more exciting and interesting when a real scandal bloomed under her nose. Yes, I can see that."

"Aunty, this isn't right!" Maggie was flushed.

"Don't bleat, my girl, and leave it to me."

"Let Mrs. Flower go on," said Gibbon.

"You're encouraging her, Inspector," complained Maggie. "She's as big a gossip as Betty Perlott ever was and you're making her worse. At her age, too."

"You forget my age, my girl, and remember that the flower stall is in my name yet. Too much nonsense from you and you'll find you'll never get it!"

Maggie retired, still muttering about age and gossips.

"She's no angel herself," said the incensed old lady. "Ask what she did when the coalman . . ."

"Aunty!"

"You haven't told me yet how Miss Perlott came to tell you the information she had picked up about the two people in Seaman's Rise. It was Seaman's Rise?"

The old lady nodded.

"I think you'd better make me a proper statement," said Winter. He looked round. The woman with red hair was edging closer to them, taking in as much as she possibly could. "Perhaps this isn't the best possible place for you to do it though, Mrs. Flower."

"If you're going to take a statement from her (and it's

enough to make a cat cry, that is, Aunty, telling the police what's true) then you'd better get her name right," said the much-goaded niece.

"Isn't it Flower?" For the first time the superintendent was taken aback.

"Argyle," said the old lady placidly. "Married Argyle. Single name Darby. Trade selling flowers for thirty-five years, so naturally I'm always called Mrs. Flower."

"And Florizel?" asked the superintendent, looking up at the name in flashing lights again. "I could have sworn there was some connection. Only coincidence?"

"My nephew."

Winter laughed. "Born Argyle?"

"Darby."

Winter turned to Maggie. "All right, Miss Darby, we needn't keep you."

"Argyle," she said hoarsely.

"No blood relation, thank goodness," said the old lady with a toss of her head.

Deciding to go with the tide Winter edged the old lady into a quiet corner, sat down beside her on a deck chair and let her talk on. He nodded to Gibbon to take unobtrusive notes.

"She wasn't a nice character, Betty Perlott. Not straight she wasn't, but that was in the family. She had a brother, well, half-brother he was really, called Bennett, and he was a real twister. I'm not sure if he didn't go to prison or to Australia or somewhere, anyway, wherever it was he died of it."

"Not prison, not Australia," said Winter under his breath; aloud he said, "I know about him. He did die."

"Yes, well, for a time I thought she was going to go like him, but she hadn't really got the brain for it and

then she got took up with one of these religious revivalists and that seemed to help her a bit. She tried to get
nicer, poor soul, I do believe, but her nature had to come
out somewhere so you see she took to all this prying and
poking and carrying of gossip. She meant well, she
said, doing the saints' work so she called it, but the
devil's *I* call it. And of course it was sex she really had
on her poor old mind (her brother was like that but *he*
found an outlet for it)."

"I see."

"Well she come to me one day, and said, 'Flo, I'm
leaving you something in my will.' Now that made me
have two thoughts. First, why should she think she
wouldn't see me out? I've got my health and spirit, I
don't deny, but I'm eighty, and don't say you don't
believe me, young man."

"Wouldn't dream of it," said Winter with some of the
new gallantry he had picked up in Paris—with anyone
of eighty surely this was safe. However, eighty was
nothing in the market and the old lady blew him a
delighted kiss.

"And then the second thing I asked myself was what
is Betty Perlott prepared to part with even before she's
dead? Something not worth having, I says to myself,
and then blow me down, if she don't come out with a
brown paper parcel and say, 'And I've got it here, only
you aren't to look at it yet, in case you should have any
difficulty laying your hands on it when I go.' So *then* I
says to myself, what is there that Betty Perlott will part
with *before* she's dead? And I answers myself straight-
away—something downright dangerous." And she
leaned back triumphant.

"And you accepted it? You've still got it?" The
superintendent leaned forward.

"It's a picture, she said to me.   A valuable one."

"You'd better let me see it," said Winter briskly.

"I can't do that."

"Why not?"

"It was burnt."   There was a minute's silence.   "As soon as I hears something has happened to Betty Perlott I knew it was on account of the picture, and I was nervous. I'd got the picture, and I knew if the person who'd helped her along came to know I'd got the picture then I'd be for it.   That's why there was a fire."

"You'd better explain a bit more, I think."

"Why was the Post Office set alight?   To burn some letters of course.   Why was my home burned?" went on Mrs. Flower who seemed to have a natural turn for the interrogative form of speech.   "Why, to burn the picture of course.   What went in the picture and the letter?   Why, something that showed two people to be no better than they should be.   It wasn't a *proper* picture, you see."   The old mouth was pursed primly.   "I was well brought up and I've kept my standards and the people in that picture weren't behaving nicely at all.   As I see it, there was a description of everything in the letter that was destroyed and the picture, which was the proof, was left with me for safety."

"Not so very safe," said Winter.   "I can see why you were frightened."

"I reckon when Betty handed that picture over to me she meant me to have a look at it.   So I did.   Gave me a bad feeling it did.   *And I recognised the faces*."   She lowered her voice.   "I let my nephew down at the art gallery have a look at it, professionally as you might say, and he said; 'Why, Aunty, it's been copied in a sort of way from the French picture of some people having a picnic.'   Some of them hadn't got nothing on.   And

205

the person who had painted the picture I had in my house had put in faces he knew, portraits you might say. Of course, they weren't very good but you could recognise them. Disgraceful, I call it. And let me tell you—it was a lot more than a picnic. Well, I don't wonder there was blackmail on account of it, yes, and murder to follow."

"Well, it was the death of Miss Perlott right enough."

"It's a judgment on her. You could see she enjoyed it in a nasty sort of way. Oh, she wasn't a straight character at all."

"It's a great pity the picture got burnt." There was a pause. "It did get burned I suppose?"

"I wasn't thinking of saving no picture when I jumped out of Cato Street, I can tell you."

"Of course not."

"Still, I'm a careful person." She looked the superintendent in the eye. "I had it photographed."

When Winter and Gibbon saw the picture they understood a great deal that previously they had only suspected.

"Dear, dear," said Winter.

"The obvious pair," said Gibbon sadly. He was not shocked. As a London policeman he had learnt about pornography long ago. "But that she should lend herself to it."

"Got a sort of pleasure out of it, I suppose," said Winter. "People do."

"Well, I can see the fuss there would be about this if it came before the wrong people."

At that moment a constable came up and muttered something. Winter put the photograph back on the table.

"We must go, Bert. There's been another death."

CHAPTER FIFTEEN

"SO HERE we are at last," said the superintendent looking down at the dead woman. "It hasn't taken so long as I thought to get here but, by God, I've seen it coming every step of the way."

The small room, it was the kitchen, was stuffy in the hot afternoon sun. The windows were not opened but someone had drawn the curtains. A fly settled on the woman's face and Gibbon brushed it away.

"How was she found?" asked the superintendent sharply. "Who discovered her and when?"

"It was the charwoman," said the constable. "Coming in to clean—she does that once a week. She found her, Mrs. Beckett."

"The second dead woman she's found lately," said Winter grimly. "Yes, I thought it would be her."

"Some people have all the luck," murmured the young constable—he was still flippant. Winter glared at him. "I doubt if she calls it that."

"She don't seem to be worrying much. Anyway, I've got her waiting for you."

"And the doctor?"

"On his way, sir."

Not that it was difficult to discover how *this* woman had died. She had been strangled with a stocking, but not perhaps one of her own, for hers, although now torn and bloody, were thin and pale, whereas the stocking round her neck was thick ugly wool, perhaps a schoolgirl's or perhaps one brought specially for the purpose. She had struggled. There was a table overturned, a torn tablecloth, clutched in desperation, shreds of it still between her fingers and under her nails.

"They always strangle," muttered the superintendent. "They always think it's going to be easy. It's not easy. Look at the room. Look at her face."

All the same she had been surprised at what had overtaken her—it was written on her face—this was not what she had expected.

Winter picked up one of her hands and examined it.

"She must have marked her murderer."

"I should think more than that must have marked him." Gibbon picked up a bottle. "Look." He held out a handful of fair hair. Gibbon still used the word "him" referring to the murderer, trying, against all the force of his reason, to convince himself that this was what he meant.

"Poor thing," said the superintendent in one of his rare moments of pity, which came to him more frequently now than perhaps they had once. "Poor thing. Young, too."

"So young? Old enough."

"A good deal must be attributed to the difference in their ages," said the superintendent thoughtfully. "Not so much but just too much."

"It's Brendan, I suppose?" One half of Bert Gibbon's mind did suppose that the murderer was Brendan, but the deeper half of his mind nourished a darker and more dreadful thought. Perhaps it wasn't Brendan, perhaps it was . . .

"He's got a burden of guilt to bear all right," agreed

the superintendent. "He's got one death behind him already. If not more," he added thoughtfully. "A man like that would do anything. D'ye know what they said about him in the army? 'A fine soldier,' his commander said, 'if he doesn't murder his best friend first.'"

"Yes, I know about the army business—he doesn't make any secret of it himself. . . ."

Winter grunted. "I didn't mean that though."

"What then? What?"

Winter grunted. "It was about seventeen years ago. Not a good time in anyone's life; 1940, just before Hamp went into the army (to do more damage there to himself and everyone). His wife left him with a man called Bennett, a man Hamp had been in business with if you can call it business; it was shady enough but still it was business to old Bennett all right—he'd got a history of that sort of racket behind him although I don't say Hamp knew this, not at first, anyway. It wasn't my case, but I knew about it, because I came into it later, almost my first case after I'd been promoted inspector it would be. Bennett was found dead in the basement air-raid shelter of his house; well, it might have been the bomb that had just dropped on his house, certainly it wasn't a time when we were going round worrying about foul play on bodies found in those circumstances and I don't suppose we'd have thought anything of it if we hadn't been looking for Bennett on our own account, and if we hadn't found the dead body of Mrs. Hamp in the same place. She'd died because she couldn't get out, she'd locked herself into a room and then the bomb had fallen and jammed up everything; she'd have been saved if someone had found her in time. We thought she might have been hiding, and it looked as though the person she was hiding from was her husband, and when we had a good look at Bennett's body it was pretty clear he'd been knocked about and not only by the bomb but before. I don't say it killed him, but if he hadn't been knocked out he'd probably have saved himself and Mrs. Hamp when the bomb fell. As it was, they both died."

"I don't call that murder quite," said Gibbon slowly.

"Brendan Hamp does though. And he isn't even *quite* sure that Bennett is dead. He can't be sure of anything, but he wonders. And then there was his wife. . . ."

"That wasn't Brendan's fault," said Gibbon sharply.

He looked down at the dead face he knew so well. He was deeply shocked.

"I suppose that this was the woman Mrs. Beckett heard on the telephone? She was responsible for killing Miss Perlott."

Winter nodded. "Largely responsible. It was because her voice was so light and unmistakably feminine that I knew Gypsy was cleared. After I heard the singing on the sands I knew that Gypsy Cresset really could never have been heard on the telephone by Mrs. Beckett without being recognised at once. *She* couldn't alter the tones of her voice."

"And now she's dead herself. Brendan Hamp?" Winter did not answer and Gibbon went on talking, thinking aloud, rationalising things to himself: "He's so proud, he'd rather kill her than have her. . . ."

Winter shrugged. "He'll swing one day, perhaps, but not for this. He didn't kill her."

"I hope you're right."

"I'm not dealing in hopes, boy, I'm dealing in facts. Why did the Post Office get burned down? Why is it that *letters* were so important? Ask yourself that, Bert, and you'll have the answer."

Gibbon raised his eyebrows in speculation.

"There's only one character off stage, Bert," said Winter impatiently. "There's your answer."

Hilary and Todd were trying to depart. They had given up using the word honeymoon for there was no honey left and even the moon was waning.

"What's this?" asked Todd seeing Buster's large obstinate face looking at him from the driving-seat. "What's he doing here?"

"He's your dog now," said Poll with pride. "You mastered him and he remembers. Isn't he clever?"

"No," said Todd. "Get out, Buster." Buster ignored this.

"I know what," said Poll, "I'll get a bone for him." She went into the house to reappear with a meaty bone. "I was saving it for Brendan's supper but never mind. Anyway, if Buster doesn't touch it (or only a lick or two, I dare say I could wash it), he can still have it."

"It'll be more than a lick," said Todd, looking respectfully at Buster's teeth. "What's Brendan going to do, chew it?"

But Buster carefully ignored the bone although an unpleasing dribble ran down his lips.

"I don't know why he doesn't want it," said Poll, squinting at it. "Seems quite a decent sort of bone, fresh and all that."

"I certainly hope so," said Brendan, "seeing that it was going to be my supper."

"Still may be, old man," said Todd, giving it a sniff. This was too much for Buster who leapt from the car with a shrill scream knocking down both his old and his new master.

"Get into the car, Hill," shouted Todd before he disappeared beneath the weight of Buster. "Get in before he can get back."

The pacification of Buster (the bone proved to be pork of which he was not fond) and the repair of Todd's ear where Buster's large canines had grazed him, took some time. Hilary and Todd went into the house to bathe his wounds and the bone was restored to the kitchen—presumably for Brendan's supper.

Afterwards no one could ever say who had been where and why and when.

Poll worked hard, helping clean Todd's car, doing a bit of gardening. She was glad to have her mind taken off things.

"I'm glad Hill's getting out of it at last," said Poll. "It'll be all over perhaps before she and Todd come back."

"I don't know what you mean." Brendan was curt.

"Oh yes you do, you've seen it coming as well as I have, haven't you? Funny thing, I was reading a book the other day that reminded me of all this. *The Trial of Constance Kent*, it was. You ever read it?"

Brendan grunted.

"It's about a Victorian family," went on Poll. "The first wife died, and the father married again. Then there was a murder in the house, a small boy, found killed and stuffed down an earth closet. Lots of people thought the father had done it."

"Don't see any resemblance to us."

"Don't you?"

"Who did do it?"

"The young sister, so she said, years later. But lots of people still thought it was Mr. Kent. Some people thought it was his new wife."

"I see."

"There was a lot of sympathy for the girl even by those who thought her guilty. People thought that she might have been upset by the second marriage—you know how adolescents are."

Brendan gave his sister a look of comprehension. "I see what you're getting at, Poll, thanks for the tip. What happened to the girl?"

"She was sent to Australia, I believe," said Poll, "but a lot of people went on believing she wasn't guilty." She added carefully, "She might have just been taking the blame."

"This hasn't been all my fault," said Brendan suddenly.

"Oh, no," said Poll, but with not much conviction.

"Thank you, sister dear, sounds as if you meant it."

Poll was silent.

"Oh, what's the good," said Brendan. "What a family we are." He paused, then almost shouted, "I killed a man once, you know."

"In the army." But Poll knew that this was not what Brendan meant.

"Well, as good as," he went on, ignoring what she had said. "I hit him on the head and no one ever saw him again. Of course he had his reasons for wanting to disappear. It was Bennett, you remember him? Well, of course you do. That's the real reason you had to go to Canada, wasn't it? You thought I didn't know, but I did."

Poll gazed at him appalled. "He was terribly attractive in a horrible sort of way," she muttered.

"Oh, I don't hold it against you. You came to your senses and got out to Canada," he said. "But you see what I mean? Not much of a family, are we? Poor Moira, if she hadn't left me for Bennett, she might have been alive now. Three days she was buried there, Poll, then on the fourth day they found her, but it was too late then. She was still alive though, and she knew me. She even spoke to me, but she looked puzzled. Yes, that was it, puzzled. I've never been the same since."

"No, I know that."

"I've never been able to forget it. In Hampstead I used to imagine people were talking about it, I could hear them all the time, and then we moved here, Poll, next door to Miss Perlott who really *did* know."

"That was just coincidence."

Brendan laughed. "Accident or coincidence? But what do you mean by those words? No, Poll, it wasn't just accident. There isn't that sort of accident. A psychologist would say that I wanted my guilt to find me out."

"You're mad."

For the first time the iron certainty that *all* events were directed at him began to crack in Brendan. Had he been wrong about the gossiping? Had he been wrong also about the cyclists and the attack on Cresta? Perhaps he would never know. He stumbled to make confession to Poll.

"I've got something to tell you, Poll. Do you remember the shop in the street off the Strand? Did you know of it in the old days? I forget now what you knew about and what you didn't. We didn't tell you everything but I think you found out a lot more than you ever told."

Poll nodded. "I knew about the shop. I followed

you there once. You used it for messages and letters and so on that it might have been dangerous to have received at home, that was it, wasn't it?"

"We weren't the only ones, you knew that, of course. It was a regular receiving centre. The Post Office, we called it, but it was more than that too. I'm pretty sure it was also a centre for the handing over of jewels, furs that were hot. A proper thieves' kitchen. The police knew of it, I suppose (although that never occurred to me then), but for some reason they never touched it. Found it useful enough themselves as a source of information, I expect. The old chap that owned it probably ran with the police as well as with the crooks."

"Wouldn't be surprised. Oh, Brendan, why didn't you keep out of it all?" But she bit back all the rest of what she wanted to say. Too late now to blame his long dead wife for all that had happened.

"Poll, I went back to the shop a little while ago. Yes, I know what you're going to say, it was a damn' foolish thing to do, still I did it. I wanted to find something out." He told Poll how he had discovered that the sharp-eyed old Perlott had remembered him, had recognised him after all this time. "I had to find out *how* she knew about the past, who she was, what her own part had been. So I had to try to find out from the papers and documents we had deposited in the shop so long ago. If they were still there. And they were. The business was still running."

He told her that he had been certain that Miss Perlott had been the sister of Mr. Bennett, the sister he just vaguely remembered, and that she had also been the typist of the letters which had passed between them. "And I found out too that she had written to have some of the papers sent down to her at Bow. Then I knew I was right in what I had feared. She was checking up on me. I hated her then, Poll."

"Look, Brendan," said Poll, "you're not telling me anything I didn't know. I knew about the Perlott. And it wasn't Miss Perlott who got in touch with the old junk shop, it was me."

"You, Poll?"

"I remember faces better than you, Brendan. I knew Miss Perlott's face as soon as I saw her. I wondered if she remembered me and if so what she could tell Bert about me. So just as you did, I thought I'd check up on the past. Our minds work alike, Brendan, the old Hamp telepathy. Maybe blood is stronger than water after all. Anyway, we both did the same thing, more fool us." Poll looked at him defiantly. "I had Bert Gibbon to think of."

"And I know what the big Hamp question is now," said Poll cynically. "Which of us is looking at a murderer?"

The garden door swung open to admit the large and solemn shapes of Superintendent Winter and Inspector Gibbon.

"Here comes Decline and Fall," said Brendan. "Now what little treat have they in store for us?"

"I'm afraid I have bad news for you," said Winter, addressing himself to Brendan in a formal fashion. "Your wife has been killed."

Brendan went very white.

"Can you tell me where your daughter and Mr. Stephen Bent are?"

"Jean and Stephen went down to the beach," muttered Brendan in a thick voice. "But Jean loves Stephen. She'd never let anything hurt him."

CHAPTER SIXTEEN

ON THEIR way to the sea front Winter and Gibbon passed by the market, which was well aware of their coming and looked at them askance. The word was well round now and the market could give a good guess about the murderer.

"You have to remember," said Winter, "that this hasn't been at all an easy case. We came at it slowly and from the wrong way round." He looked at Brendan who was trudging wearily by his side. Brendan had insisted on coming, because Jean was, after all, his daughter, although he looked forward to the approaching moment with horror and despair. "You, Mr. Hamp, made it difficult for us by insisting that the emphasis was really upon you. You distorted the picture one way just as Mr. Todd distorted it another. Well, we've got that cleared up."

Brendan grunted. He wouldn't speak.

"The very first question that faced us was: did we have a case at all? Had Miss Perlott been murdered? And with that went the question, how? The answer to one was the answer to the other. She had been cunningly murdered. But it was a give-away murder. The person who could plan that sort of scientific, careful yet artful murder wasn't after all going to be so hard to recognise. Proof was different. There are what I call indications— the cat was one. Who would kill the cat in that way?

Only a cold practical scientific soul. There were two people in the killing. You've grasped that by now?"

"There's science and science," answered Brendan.

"Then there was the affair, if I may call it that, of Miss Cresta Cresset. What exactly was that? Was it an accident, was it an attack aimed at Miss Cresset, or as you said, Mr. Hamp, one aimed at you? I very soon came to the conclusion it was a genuine accident. But what was she doing in your house? And once again I came to the conclusion that she was, perfectly innocently, looking for her sister. You were all out in the road, remember. But the reason she had to find her sister so urgently wasn't perhaps so innocent."

"We know about that now."

"Then there was the explosion—the double explosion as it turned out. And, of course, that is what gave the murderer away. Why was there an explosion? Because Miss Perlott, who thought she was going to be married as a reward for information received had duly written a letter. The letter had to be destroyed. And how better than by destroying all the letters posted in that area that day. The Cato Street fire was also meant to destroy something. But the explosions revealed that the murderer had not only access to explosives but also to the sort of detonating agent used in mines. The details were narrowing down."

He looked at Brendan. "You want to know, don't you? It's as well you should. You'll have to talk to your daughter. Then there was the speed of the laying of the explosions. Did the murderer have wings? No, but there was a bicycle to be used. You were all misled there. Anyone could have used it, of course. It was openly around."

Brendan wiped his face.

"You see it all? I can see you do. The motive is hard on you, but love, of this kind, is a ruthless and destroying and selfish thing. It didn't really matter to this person who got hurt. It was a progressive thing though. And it got nastier. And when there was a definite attempt to implicate an innocent person, the end was near."

Jean and Stephen were walking among the crowds. But it seemed to Jean that they were known and marked as having come from the street where there had been murder. She could hear whispers and feel eyes upon them.

"I ought to go back," she said uneasily.

"I don't think so. Don't go yet. So much to talk about. You were laughing and gay a little while ago. Why have you suddenly grown so quiet?"

For Jean was quiet.

There were some things, she thought, that she would not talk about, even to Stephen. Perhaps in a little time she would forget what had happened, and once forgotten perhaps it would be as if they had never happened. "And maybe not," said the irrepressible Hamp rising to the surface in her. She kicked violently at one of the pebbles on the beach.

"You're strong," said Stephen. "Here, let's sit down. You're a clever girl, Jean."

Still she kept her tongue still.

"Clever and strong." His voice was admiring. "You're the cleverest in your family, I reckon. Except perhaps for dear old Poll—she's as fly as they come, much good has it done her."

"That was a funny thing to say," said Jean reluctantly.

"Was it? Was it? *You* know better than that."

A wind blew in from the sea lifting the heat and rustling the newspapers. Jean shivered.

"Don't be afraid," said Stephen gently.

"I'm not afraid," said Jean. "Not of you. You're afraid of me, I think." She was sad. "And I love you, Stephen, I really do."

"You're so clever," said Stephen, "so strong and clever you see—it's dangerous."

Jean laughed. "No Hamp is dangerous," she said.

"There isn't one of you that isn't. You're full of violence and energy. That's what attracts me, I suppose."

"But not to me," said Jean. "Not to me, not to me."

"You can't get over that, can you? That's what I mean about you Hamps."

"Unjust," muttered Jean.

"A woman scorned, eh, Jean?"

"Oh, you're being unkind."

"Yes it was, and rude. I apologise. I don't know what's the matter with me." He picked up a handful of pebbles and began to drop them one by one through his fingers. "Yes, I do though. I need to talk to you."

"Supposing I won't?" said Jean, turning away. "There's absolutely no reason why I should."

"I know what you're going to do, Jean. I've seen it coming, I've seen it in your face. I couldn't believe it at first, not of *you*, but it's true all the same. I am convinced."

"Don't shout."

"You'll go to the police, won't you, Jean?"

The wind had dropped and nothing disturbed the hot calm of the beach. In the distance children shouted in the sea and an old dog barked.

"Well, won't you? It would make it easier for you."

"Nothing could do that."

"Still, you've been thinking that you might go to the police. I can see it in your face. Don't cry."

"I'm not crying."

"And after all they might not take any notice of you. It's only what you *think*, isn't it? Do stop crying. Ruth didn't cry."

Jean looked up at him.

"No, she didn't cry. She was surprised though."

"What have you done, Stephen?"

"It was a shame about Ruth," said Stephen in a conversational way. "She had to try and get away from London. People had started to talk. Called her a nymphomaniac. She was a bit of one perhaps, but what of it? She didn't have much trouble in persuading Brendan to move because he'd heard talk too, although, poor old thing, he thought it was all directed at *him*. He thought it was because of . . . I suppose I ought not to talk about this in front of you."

"Oh, don't be delicate now. I suppose you mean Dad thought it was all about him and Mother and what happened years ago. He thinks we don't know." Jean's voice was strained and exhausted.

"Yes, well, we all know really, don't we? He thought it was about him, all this talk, only, of course, it wasn't. He just had a guilty conscience."

"Just say a conscience."

"Put it how you like. Anyway, as soon as you all moved here Miss Perlott popped up into the picture and she really was in a position to talk about your father because she was half-sister to the man Bennett who took your mother away with him and who, of course, started that rather stupid fraud in the first place (Brendan was a fool, I'd never let myself in for anything like that). But the really tiresome thing was that she found out about me and Ruth and was going to tell my father. I was frightened. He's got quite a nice little bit of money tucked away and he's no chicken. I've only got to wait, you see. So I fixed her. Quite easy to do. I read all about it in a newspaper. And, of course, I knew about the weak heart. Sometimes I wonder why I didn't just frighten her to death. But the other way was cleverer, wasn't it?"

"Oh, much."

"Don't be bitter. Doesn't suit you. And then I discovered she'd already sent the letter to my father. The silly old thing expected him to marry her. So I arranged the little fire at the Post Office. That was masterly, you know. I used some of my father's mining explosive there. Quite ironic, don't you think?"

"And what about Cato Street?"

"Well, would you believe it, the old vixen Perlott had stolen a picture I was painting of me and Ruth. I won't go into it, but it was one that you might call 'special'."

"Like the one I saw you had torn up?"

"That's right," said Stephen, with what was almost a grin. "Clever girl. You'll be the death of me yet." He laughed. "Oh well, it's all over now. Poor Ruth. Still, what I did was the kindest thing. She had to go bravely."

"Stephen, what have you done?"

"You know it's hardest of all on your father, I quite see that. I'm not altogether heartless, in fact I've got too much heart, that's been the trouble. But after all he will keep marrying the wrong sort—oh, sorry, wrong thing to say. You might think it was an accident but it isn't really. Not accident, not coincidence. If he had thirty wives they'd all be the same; he's looking out for that sort of thing, he wants to be tormented. I've worked it all out. So, you see, I wasn't to blame. Nor was Ruth, poor girl."

"Stephen, where is she?"

"I did it all for you. I discovered she was going all for laying it on you. I couldn't have that. Besides, she was losing her head. So I strangled her. There's no need to cry so much." He paused and looked out to sea dreamily. "Oh, but she was lovely. Lovely," he repeated with a little laugh.

"Oh why, why, Stephen, why all of this, why kill at all, for such little reasons really?"

"But I've told you. Oh well, I guess Brendan was right. We're that sort of people, me and Ruth, we're just the murdering kind."

"I liked her, I did," sobbed Jean. "She was good to us. She made us a family."

"Yes, she was a good sort was Ruth," said Stephen. "But there you are, there was all the rest too."

He looked up towards the crowded esplanade. Through the crowd he could see Superintendent Winter and Inspector Gibbon approaching.

"Here they come," he said. "They've found her. Better get up, Jean, you don't want to be with me when it happens. Go on, get in right with them. Go and tell them what I've been saying." She paused, looking at him with eyes full of pain. "Go on, tell them. They won't hang me, you know, I'm too young."

So Jean, not without many a backward look at the beloved figure sitting on the beach letting the pebbles drip through his fingers in the familiar fashion, walked slowly to where she could see the two policemen coming down the steps.

"So there won't be a happy ending after all, Bert," said Winter a little sadly. "Not the way you wanted it."

"Oh, I don't know," answered Gibbon. "There's one for Jean, if she'll see it. She'll go to college now, and make something of herself. She's clever and she's brave."

"True enough."

"And then there's Poll, she's got the vitality for six, she'll pull through, and I'll help her, if she'll let me. It could have come out worse. There's Brendan, of course." He paused. "Perhaps he'll always be the same. If he had ten wives, they would always be the wrong sort."

"I didn't know you saw it so clear, Bert."

"The real tragedy is Stephen Bent, the silly stupid boy. It's funny how mistaken we all were in him; we thought he was so spontaneous and romantic and charming and the spontaneity was merely selfishness, and the romanticism was sensuousness and the charm was the result of a complete egotism. Beneath it all was murder."